CONNECTION TERMINATED

TANAY PANT

Joshua Tree Publishing

• Chicago •

Connection Terminated
Tanay Pant

Published by
Joshua Tree Publishing
• Chicago •
JoshuaTreePublishing.com

13-Digit Print ISBN: 978-1-956823-33-2
13-Digit Print eBook: 978-1-956823-34-9

Front Cover Image Credit: Submarine © Marko
                            Background: © Rawpixel.com

Disclaimer:
This is a work of fiction. Names, characters, places, and incidents are the product of the author's imagination or have been used fictitiously. Any resemblance to actual persons, living or dead, events, locales or organizations is entirely coincidental.

Printed in the United States of America

DEDICATED TO YOU,

THE READER.

CHAPTER ONE

TROOPERS

A beam of sunlight struck the interior of a wooden room before ricocheting off and striking Elijah square in the eyes. He had been dozing dreamlessly for well over nine hours, which was odd, considering rest wasn't something he was used to. Eyes fluttering open and closed, he put a wobbly elbow under his body and slowly pulled himself out of bed. Sunlight had nearly illuminated his entire room, delivering a cozy and warm feeling similar to that of a wooden fireplace at night. Elijah took a deep breath, held it for a moment, then let it out with a massive sigh. Not an ounce of stress burdened him.

His eyes peered out the glass pane to his left and rested on a garden of bright flowers and trees. Birds of all kinds chirped a song that, accompanied by the beauty of nature he was surrounded with, gave Elijah indescribable bliss. Still, as he bounced to his heels, smiling to himself and looking out the window at the mesmerizing natural beauty, he felt, oddly enough, like something was . . . off. Despite the wonderful view and calming melody of the birds, he felt his stomach stir in anxiety.

He didn't have a chance to put all of his thoughts together before the plants outside started to droop, then wither. Confused, he looked up and saw that the sun had turned a frigid blue hue, like the moon on a cold winter night. The singing of the birds became persistently louder, no longer soft and natural. Their mellow caws of unrhythmic melody morphed into a consistent soulless noise that threatened to drive him insane.

Caw. Caw. Screech. Screech.

Elijah grimaced and fell backward with a forceful thump. Had he not been in shock, he may have noticed how unbearably cold the room was getting. The wood that once surrounded him turned slushy and fell apart like gravel. Shivering, Elijah lifted his hand and scooped out a piece of the wall. His suspicions were proven correct: the walls had turned into snow. He curled up into a fetal position, jaw shaking uncontrollably, and started gasping from the freezing temperature. Tears streamed down his eyes as he grappled with the absurdity of his situation. The birds wouldn't stop. They kept repeating the same beeping and screeching they had before, and with each screech, the noise became more deliberate and deafening.

Caw. Beep. Screech. Beep.

"Jesus, Elijah, get UP, " quipped a voice from behind.

Startled, he jolted up, smashing his head on a hanging piece of wood from the ceiling in the process. His vision was blurred, but he could make out the person who had spoken to him, as well as a clock on a table nearby. The noise, however, wouldn't stop.

Beep. Beep. Beep. Beep.

A fist slammed down on the alarm clock, ceasing the beeping immediately.

"God, I hate that thing," she muttered as she massaged her hand.

She turned back to Elijah, who had finally woken up most of his basic brain function. Ignoring the pain on the side of his head, he surveyed the room. Poorly kept bunk beds? Some kind of war insignia on the wall? A familiar-looking girl smirking at his dumbfounded face?

Oh yeah, that's right. Elijah was in the Navy.

One huff later, Elijah hopped off his bed and started collecting his thoughts. The blanket he had been wearing was torn off onto the ground; it appeared to have been tampered with less than a minute ago.

Huh, that plus the clock? That explains the nightmare, he thought.

He turned to the girl, unamused.

"Christ, Laila," he sighed, "can't I have just one good night's rest down here? That's all I ask, really."

She smiled innocently, but it was obvious she enjoyed watching him make a fool out of himself.

"No, apparently not," she joked, grabbing a jacket and throwing it directly at his face. "What was it this time?"

Elijah used one hand to claw the jacket off his face and the other to rub his temple.

"I don't know, I just had it. I think . . . I was back in New Mexico? The same little mansion with the whole garden and prairie thing. I mean, that was before you tore off the blanket and made me go to an arctic nightmare," he scoffed. "Just because we're in the Navy doesn't mean everything has to be rough, okay?"

Laila laughed heartily. "We do everything rough *because* we're in the Navy, idiot. Now get dressed, you're late for the meeting in Mess, and Commander Patrick said he had something special planned for us today. Besides, what kind of example would an AP student be setting by showing up late?"

"My bad, I forgot that you're an obedient conformist to everyone else in this place," he scoffed as he tugged his uniform on. The Insignia of the Navy could be seen under his left breast pocket, with the initials 'A.P.' off on the side of the coat. *Accelerated Performance.*

Elijah groaned as he stretched his leg against the stump of his bed.

"I don't understand how you can be such a jerk only to me and then put on your little goody-goody facade anytime you see a commander."

"A real mystery, isn't it?" she snickered before disappearing out the door. "And you owe me one for getting you up on time!"

She was right about that, he had to admit. She did just save his butt by getting him up before the major meeting CDR Patrick was planning. Plus, despite being an infuriating clown sometimes, she was a genuine friend of his. Lord knows that with him seeing none of his friends after high school, her signing up for this specific naval program and getting put in the same squad as him was a miracle. A familiar face in all this chaos was what he needed at the moment, and he was glad she was here.

Still, Elijah thought. *It wouldn't kill her to take it easy sometimes.*

After a fit of annoyed muttering, Elijah put on his shoes, tugged on his collar, and raced after her to the mess hall. She showed him today, but he wouldn't let her get bragging rights for being first, too. As he ran down the stairs, he wondered: what could CDR Patrick possibly have in mind for them? The Accelerated Performance program had always been about the new tests they wanted to try on advanced crew, but until now that just meant more rigorous training and harder workouts. Would they finally get a chance to do something new? Something interesting?

Upon turning the corner, Elijah caught sight of a disheveled-looking boy with red hair up ahead. His hair was unkempt and wild, his shirt untucked, and his breath heavy with what was likely the most demanding workout he had gotten all week. Elijah grinned as he saw him speed-walk to the best of his ability down the hall.

"Hey, Sebastian!" he called out. The boy turned, almost tripping over himself in the process. "Where's your sister?"

"Debra's already at the hall," Sebastian gasped. His speech was stifled by a mouthful of toast that he had likely grabbed on his way to the hall. Still running, his eyes narrowed as he noticed Elijah's absent-minded grin. "What're you smiling at?"

Elijah snapped back to reality. "Oh, nothing. It's just . . ." he sighed and shrugged his shoulders. "It's been a funny morning, is all."

Sebastian shrugged, having already lost interest before Elijah could finish. "You were also called by Patrick, weren't you? What do you think he has planned for us?"

"I'm not entirely sure," Elijah responded.

Truth be told, he wasn't particularly fond of talking to Sebastian. While he was fully aware that he could be a bit of a jerk himself (in retrospect a bit too much), he still thought that Sebastian was an insufferable person in general. He couldn't put his finger on why, either, which made it more frustrating to explain why he disliked him. Regardless, it wasn't important right now. He shook his head before picking up his pace. "See you soon, League."

"Yeah," he huffed, "whatever."

As corridors passed, Elijah began taking in more and more of his surroundings. Steel blocks lined every wall, with windows peering out now and then to a vast, brown wetland filled with ponds and other buildings for his station. A dark sky and darker clouds loomed overhead, inviting another day of torrential downpour. Ever since Elijah's parents had forced him into the Navy, he hadn't gotten a good long look at what surrounded him and his friends. It seemed like he was always caught up in something else.

He stopped running for a minute to catch his breath and peered out a window. He thought he could see a tiny frog hop off the roof of a nearby shed into a pond that had formed from the rain the night before. Puddles surrounded the area, contrasting with the mud and ridiculous amount of wet marsh. It was a scene completely juxtaposed to that of his home in New Mexico, where his parents had owned a magnificent wooden house in a gated community, surrounded by lush green forests and the occasional patch of desert. His school, where he met Laila years ago, had every opportunity for Elijah to grow up to be whatever he chose. Engineer? Doctor? Perhaps an entrepreneur, if he so chose? As it turns out, it would be none of those things. Elijah thought back to about a year ago . . .

"We've talked about this, Elijah," his mother scolded. This was way back when Elijah still thought he had a chance to go to college without any hiccups. "Your father and I both served in the military. So did your grandparents. As did your great-grandparents. I understand if you want to pursue some vain degree at university sometime in the future, but you can't go until you do what your forefathers and mothers have done for years."

"She's right," said his father. His voice was far deeper and concentrated. It cracked through the air like a whip, striking Elijah's ears and smashing his hopes with spectacular efficiency.

"Our family is molded around service. You may not go to college until you've served at least a year or two. AH—"

Elijah's dad stopped him before he could even murmur a syllable of discontent, "—that is final." A humph, a turn, and both his parents walked out of his room in unison. In less than a minute, his life path was set off completely.

Now look, ranted Elijah inwardly. *I get to be rolled out of bed by a roommate who's my only semblance of home, running through wet corridors in a building crawling with bugs, surrounded by mud, dirt, insects, and—*

"ELI!" shouted a high voice from behind, followed by a smack to Elijah's head. His forehead smashed against the mushy brick wall before bouncing back like a bobo doll. "How's it going?"

Elijah rubbed his forehead and, despite himself, chuckled slightly. Then, without hesitation, he pushed his elbow backward in the voice's direction, striking their stomach and prompting a gasp from the recipient of the blow. Elijah laughed harder and turned around. Yup. It was exactly as he expected.

"Get up, Rohan," Elijah smiled, reaching his arm out to the boy wheezing on the floor. Reluctantly, Rohan grabbed on and lifted himself.

"You good?" questioned Elijah, his smile unwavering.

Rohan lifted a finger, the other hand placed on his stomach, continuing to take deep breath after deep breath. Finally, he looked up at Elijah.

"JESUS, Eli!" he sputtered, gasps still billowing out his body. "You don't have to hit me *that* hard."

Elijah grinned more.

"Aww, it's almost been half a year, and you still can't handle an elbow to the stomach? Why the hell did you sign up for the Navy if you couldn't handle a middle-school-grade fight tactic?"

Rohan waved his hand, motioning for Elijah to stop talking.

"It didn't—" he stopped talking for a second and took a long breath yet again, hands glued to his abdomen. "It . . . It didn't even hurt—that bad," he finally croaked out before leaning against the wall again.

Elijah beamed. That was Rohan, alright. This wasn't some isolated incident, either. Elijah could recall at least three different times that Rohan had tried to catch Elijah off guard, only to end up on the carpet, cursing. The first time was objectively the best, though. It also happened to be the first time they met.

Following hours of waiting and a bumpy sleepless bus ride, Elijah and the other recruits had finally arrived at the compound a little past 2:00 a.m. The commanders had had enough mercy on them to allow them to sleep for a full night one last time before training started. Elijah vividly recalled how he dragged his weak body through the halls, willing with all his might to crash onto a bed and sleep uninterrupted for weeks. His boots were soaked, his eyes refused to stay open, and he didn't even think to get out of his uniform before dropping. His zombie-like classmates showed up minutes later, and he finally heaved a sigh of relief. He was just about ready to fall into a dreamless coma before he felt a push on his shoulder.

"Move, dude," came a sluggish voice from behind. "I wanna sleep on the top."

Elijah couldn't believe what he was hearing. *I've got to be hallucinating,* he thought. It was the only explanation. There was simply no way a Navy recruit was pushing another off the top bunk of a bed at 2:00 a.m. just because he didn't want to sleep on the bottom.

"Go to sshleep," Elijah managed to hiss out. But the poking didn't stop.

"I always sleep on the top back home," the voice continued. "Come on, man, just move."

This is a joke, he reasoned. *A stunt. Not a very fun one, though.* He sighed audibly.

"Stop poking me or you're sleeping on the ground."

The poking continued.

"Dude, for the love of God, take the bottom bunk. It's two in the morning."

The poking stubbornly continued.

Feeling the frustration boil closer and closer to the brim, Elijah finally had enough. With what little energy he could muster, he swung his leg out from under the blanket and knocked the voice in the chin. A yelp later, the recipient of the kick collapsed onto the ground and groaned for a full minute, spilling enough obscenities to last a lifetime. Minutes later, victory was achieved as he crawled into the bottom bunk, curses still spilling. Sleep came fast after that.

The next morning, Elijah was walking down the halls of the building, trying desperately to remember how to get to the mess hall. Laila had gotten up early, and he knew she would already be there, ready to mock him for his terrible memory. There was no chance of her being tardy on the first day, that's for sure. On his way, he saw a brown-skinned kid stumbling along, looking just as lost as Elijah.

"Hey," Elijah called out.

The kid turned around, flustered. "Hi."

Elijah recognized the voice and narrowed his brow.

"Did you try to wrestle someone for top bunk yesterday at two in the morning?"

The boy stopped moving and avoided eye contact. "Maybe. Did you kick someone in the chin at two in the morning because of a harmless question?"

Elijah scoffed. *Harmless question, his ass.*

"Maybe."

The kid nodded. As they turned the corner, they could begin to hear the faint noise of a hundred kids packed into a cafeteria talking and eating. Elijah looked at the kid.

"What's your name?"

The kid looked back. "It's Rohan."

Elijah nodded. "You're a complete moron, you know that?"

"Shut up," he responded with no hesitation.

Still, Elijah swore that a grin flickered on and off his face unwillingly.

Elijah smiled. This guy was a clown, for sure, but he had a friendly aura around him. It kinda felt like home, in a weird way.

"Let's go," he said. "We'll miss breakfast."

And without needing to look, Elijah knew that Rohan was following, a grin forming on his face, already plotting how he was going to get his revenge.

Chapter Two

Briefing

Back in the present, Elijah was still chuckling to himself over Rohan's idiocy when a bell started ringing throughout the halls. *Crap,* Elijah thought, finding the situation less amusing. *That's the late bell!*

Leaving Rohan hacking, he continued running down to the mess hall. He cursed himself for spending so much time laughing at Rohan. *What would it look like if he was late to the first major project in the AP program?*

He raced towards the clamor of voices, just two or three turns away. His foot caught a loose piece of the metal floor, tripping him up, but still, he pushed forward. Finally, he burst into the hall, with thousands of rugged and mischievous young adults eating, gossiping, and catching up on much-needed sleep. Nothing unusual there.

He turned his head to the right and saw a large curtain separating the mass number of recruits in Mess from the AP candidates. He parkoured between the passing recruits like an acrobat and pulled back the curtain just as a bell rang overhead. With a bright red face, aching legs, and a side stitch bad enough to get him out of the daily 5k, he collapsed into a seat and tried to not breathe too hard. If everyone didn't know better, they'd take one look at him and assume he had just summited a mountain. When he looked up, he saw every single person in the room, including CDR Brookes and Patrick, staring directly at him, with Laila being the only one laughing her head off. Great. Flawless introduction right there.

CDR Brookes busied herself setting up a projector for the lesson, so CDR Patrick was the first to speak.

"Alright, everyone," he thundered.

Everyone in the room instinctively flinched from the volume of Patrick's voice. Matter of fact, Elijah couldn't recall a time the man wasn't speaking like he was presenting in a crowded theater.

"You all know that something big is going on, and you're not wrong at all. Some of you," he said, leaning his head in Elijah's direction, "seem to be ecstatic to hear all about it."

A few chuckles rose out of the audience but were quickly silenced by a clap from Patrick.

"Enough. You should notice that very few of your fellow AP students are here today. That is because you ten . . ." he trailed off.

Everyone swiveled in their chair, put off by the sudden halt of speech until they counted in the room and realized that there were only eight people.

Patrick grunted, unimpressed, "Well, I guess some people won't be—"

"I'M HERE!!" A desperate voice called out as it crashed through the curtain. Rohan.

Elijah didn't know whether to laugh, cry, or shake his head in shame. Did he not know anything about how to act? If you're late, you slink quietly into the room when no one's looking, not barge in like a drunk SWAT officer.

"Ah." Patrick's gaze lasered onto Rohan's, who swiftly took a seat and tried to pretend like the last ten seconds didn't happen.

A few moments later, Sebastian, toast crumbs all over his hands, barged in as well. "Sorry I'm late—"

"Shut up and sit down. We don't have time for this."

Sheepishly, he obeyed.

"Okay. That's everyone," he grunted and grabbed a remote, gazing at CDR Brookes. She looked up from her laptop and gave a thumbs up. Patrick nodded and looked back at the recruits.

"Now. Without any more interruptions, here's what you're here for.

"You are all here as AP students because we have a new program for you to attempt. A real-world simulation, if you will. You've been chosen from the grandiose pool of applicants because you are either physically fit, intellectually applicable, or you were simply chosen via lottery. Take a look around you," he said, motioning with his hand to look around the room. "See who you will be embarking on this project with."

Following everyone else's example, Elijah craned his head to look around the room. He spotted Laila and Rohan immediately, to which he inwardly celebrated. If he was going to be undertaking some groundbreaking project, there were few other people he'd rather do it with than those two. He continued looking around, counting off some other peers he'd seen before. He spotted Sebastian again, still huffing from the run to the hall, sitting next to his younger sister, Debra. She looked frantic, gazing around the room in a panicked daze as if she had just downed a dozen energy drinks before coming here.

Poor girl, Elijah thought. *She probably doesn't get to sleep much with all the work she does.*

He'd seen both her and Sebastian in the technical ward several times, messing around with dials and wires as mini-projects when they weren't running around and learning what stance to take when a commander enters the room. Yeah, they were nerds, but Elijah could tell they were good at what they did. Nobody would ever hunch over all that tech for hours at a time unless they knew what they were doing. Plus, it seemed that tech was the one thing Sebastian genuinely enjoyed doing. His sister, on the other hand, always looked far too exhausted to have any joy in her work.

Not far away was Lars. Elijah also recognized him from the ward, guiding the League siblings and acting as their mentor in a way. He was easily the eldest non-commander in the room, maybe twenty-ish, and he had a thick German accent. Elijah hadn't had many conversations with him, and whenever he did, they would only last for a minute or two at a time. He seemed like the type of guy to keep to himself.

There were a few other AP students scattered around the room, too. Elijah was surprised he recognized so many, like Cassidy, a tall blonde girl who looked drowsy and uninterested in what was going on around her. Elijah recognized her as the girl who always got in trouble with the higher-ups for blatantly ignoring orders until they were ready to snap with impatience. Laila once mentioned a time when CDR Patrick screamed at her in front of everyone for not getting up on time, to which she got out of bed, walked right past him, and went to the bathroom before locking the door. All without acknowledging that Patrick was even there. Elijah flinched at that memory. Laila said she had never seen someone's temples flare that much in rage. No chance that Patrick picked her to come along. She must've gotten lucky with the lottery.

It was a bit dark from the back of the room, so Elijah couldn't see the other three kids. He was ready to get up and look when CDR Patrick clapped his hands again, making everyone jump.

"That's more than enough time," he declared. "Now onto the actual project." He waved his hand towards CDR Brookes, who smiled and stepped onto the stage.

Subconsciously, a smile spread across Elijah's face as well. He liked Brookes far more than Patrick. She knew when to relax and lay off the screaming, while Patrick seemed to always have his head in military mode.

Brookes snatched the remote from Patrick's hand as he walked off to the side of the curtain, fidgeted around with the buttons for a bit, and then began.

"First off, if any of y'all saw the submarine outside . . ." there were murmurs of agreement and acknowledgment from the recruits, " . . . good. Y'all are all getting in that thing the day after tomorrow."

Elijah's jaw involuntarily dropped. Laila let out a small squeal before immediately covering her mouth.

Brookes sighed and continued, "Yeah, yeah, it's a big deal. But don't think you're going to be on your own fighting the Chinese or something. CDR Patrick and I will be accompanying you on this project."

A hand shot out of the audience.

"Yes, Cassidy?" Brookes asked.

"Yeah, uh," Cassidy yelled, oblivious to the hushed environment around her, "what exactly is this project about? And what does that have to do with being on a submarine?"

"She's getting to that," Patrick thundered, glaring directly at Cassidy.

It was obvious that he was tired of her, and Elijah couldn't help but wonder if he silently objected to her being here. Cassidy didn't bat an eye at his comment.

"Well, Cassidy," Brookes continued, also unphased by Patrick's outburst, "as AP recruits, y'all haven't been doing much of anything different than the rest. Maybe more laps around the pond, but that's about it. Today, we want y'all to prove yourselves as truly advanced recruits. You will all embark on a Class N submarine with CDR Patrick and me ten miles off the coast and thousands of feet deep. From there, you'll have to complete a series of tasks to radio up to the surface, as well as guide the submarine back up. Patrick and I will accompany you because, well, none of y'all have been on the inside of a submarine before, and I have a feeling one of you is going to screw something up big time." She smiled a bit. "And I'll be damned if I let almost a dozen immature recruits onto a submarine by themselves. Better to have us down there to watch over y'all."

Several different thoughts raced through Elijah's mind. They were going in a submarine? An actual, real-life, physical submarine? Two-thousand feet underwater? He turned around to see the reaction of the others. Laila was looking at him, eyes wide and mouth agape in disbelief. Rohan's leg bounced uncontrollably as he stared at the ceiling, his breath picking up speed. The Leagues' looked like they were going to burst from excitement, Lars had a wide grin spread across his face, and Cassidy, against all odds, actually looked somewhat interested.

Laila began to raise her hand but was cut off by a silencing hand motion by Brookes.

"Keep your questions until after I finish talking," she said, not unkindly. "Now, this is going to be a massive leap from anything you've done so far, but if you complete it properly, you will solidify your position in the AP program—and maybe even graduate early from your recruitment training. At least, that's the plan. But what is certain," she elaborated, her voice slowly becoming more stern, "is that this is something to be taken seriously. If you think you're going to get away with horseplay or some unfunny prank in a submarine deep underwater, you can kiss your ass goodbye from the AP program now and—if I get my way—the Navy entirely. I hope that's made clear because I sure as hell am not repeating myself."

On the other side of the room, CDR Patrick nodded in agreement. The rest of the recruits shuffled around in their chairs, still in disbelief that they were going on a mission of this magnitude.

Up ahead, Laila once again raised her hand, to which Brookes sighed and called on her.

"Umm, I, I don't know," Laila stammered, unable to form a coherent sentence from the clear shock she was in. "I guess, what I mean to say, is, um, what . . ." she paused. "What if something goes wrong? Like, not part of the project, but what if something goes wrong with the submarine?"

Brookes chuckled in response.

"Laila," she started, "we'll be down there with you. Mr. Arnold here," she said as she motioned to a man behind the curtain, who revealed himself upon hearing his name, "will be up above with Officer Zane to look after y'all the entire time you're down there. The radio won't be broken," she said as she rolled her eyes, as though it were the most obvious thing in the world, "but it will be disconnected to the point where you'll have some sort of experience with repairing broken items on a ship. Again, it's just a simulation of lost contact, no one's actually cutting all ties with the surface and expecting y'all to figure it out."

There was silence among the recruits, save for the frantic breathing of a few of them, before Cassidy lazily put her hand in the air.

"Question," she exclaimed in a monotone voice. "Is all of this done yet?"

Brookes stared at her, impatience boiling behind her eyes.

"Yes. Your bags are already filled up in your room, but if you want to throw in a book or something to keep yourself occupied during the non-project hours of the transit, be my guest. Just be ready the day after tomorrow at 0700 to board." She gazed around the room. "Got it?"

Cassidy immediately jolted up and left without a word of acknowledgment, prompting both of the commanders to shake their heads and groan.

Everyone else, with varying degrees of enthusiasm, repeated "Yes ma'am" as they got out of their seats.

Elijah stood, fixed his shirt collar, and looked around. He first caught Laila's eye, then Rohan's. Immediately, they all grinned and started pacing out of the room, ready to mull over the events that had just unfolded. After all, there were only three hours left until lunch, and there was a lot to talk about.

CHAPTER THREE

COMPANIONS

Elijah could do little to stifle his excitement for lunch. All of his drills—including the dreaded daily 5k run—were over. He had showered, changed, and prepared his bag for tomorrow's project. Mess hall was set to open in around five minutes, and then he, Rohan, and Laila could chatter endlessly about the mission.

However, the more Elijah sat and stirred in anticipation, the more he felt that he was missing something. He spent a moment or two dwelling on it, wondering what he could possibly be missing, before realizing what it was. Quickly, he jumped up onto his bunk and reached his hand underneath his pillow, hoping to hear the familiar click-clack of tablets clattering around a container.

Nothing.

Elijah reached farther in, sweeping his arm side-to-side to scan the entire underside of the pillow.

Still nothing.

Elijah's heart started to thump faster. With sweaty palms, he lifted his pillow to reveal a distinct lack of pills anywhere on his bunk. The weight of the situation began to settle on his shoulders, sending a wave of anxiety through his body with each passing minute. His arms shook as he brought the pillow back down onto his bed, climbing down on his hands and knees to search around the room. Struggling to keep his breathing under control, he hurled pillows off nearby bunks and scattered around the room in a frenzy, eyes darting everywhere in search. He was on the verge of a panicked breakdown when he noticed a gleam of light reflecting off of an orange cylindrical bottle just behind one of the wooden legs that kept all the bunks up. Elijah scrambled towards it and inspected the label, after which he exhaled heavily, unaware that he had been holding his breath. He grasped the bottle between two of his fingers and shook it back and forth, allowing the clatter of objects from the bottle to drown out his fading anxiety. His sleeping pills. He had no idea what he'd do without them.

For as long as he could remember, Elijah had always had intense trouble sleeping. He was incredibly fortunate that his parents were used to getting little sleep—being in the army and all—because according to them, he was NOT a fun baby to put to bed. They dismissed it as childhood shenanigans at the time, but their attitude switched when he started falling asleep constantly in class and had to be sent to the disciplinary office every other day for not being able to keep his eyes open. Elijah flinched recalling those memories. It was difficult to forget the look on his father's face when he found out his "model son" wasn't acting up to his standards. Finally, when he was around fifteen years old and almost fell asleep during his first driving test, his parents caved and took him to a pediatrician who prescribed him the pills that he had taken every other night since then. If he went more than two days without popping at least one pill, he wouldn't get a wink of sleep at night, which was especially important considering his program wasn't particularly lenient on sleep schedules.

Elijah looked back at the pill bottle one last time before clawing open his bag and stashing the bottle in the folds of an extra pair of clothes he was bringing for the trip. For some reason that he still cursed himself over to that day, he had lied on his recruitment form and said that he didn't need any special medication at camp. He thought that saying that he was dependent on a bunch of capsules would make him seem fragile, unfit for the AP program or even the Navy entirely. So, since his recruitment a half year ago, he had been rationing and hiding his pills in different locations to ensure that no one found out that he was taking them. Only Laila knew, and that was because she was the one who forced him to stand up to his parents at fifteen and ask to see a doctor about his condition.

Elijah sighed as he plopped himself back on the ground, still recovering from the anxiety he had just undergone. There were only about eight pills left in that bottle. Maybe enough to get him through the next two weeks, tops. He had no idea where he would get more, but that was the least of his problems at the moment. The project ahead of him occupied him far more than his insomnia did.

A bell overhead interrupted his thoughts and signaled that it was time for lunch. Elijah collected himself and threw his bag onto his bunk. He walked out of the room, down the stairs, then down the halls that led to the mess hall. For once, he didn't need to sprint through the entire compound to make it on time. He took note of how nice it was to take a relaxing stroll for once. Finally, when he got to the hall, he threw open the doors and searched for his companions.

The Leagues were sitting alone at a table in the back, with Sebastian chowing down on beans and rice while helping his sister, Debra, with something on a laptop. As usual, she looked like she had just guzzled enough energy drinks to keep her awake for weeks on end. Elijah started to wonder why Lars wasn't helping them like usual before seeing a hand wave at him across the room. Laila and Rohan were already settled and were waving at him to come over. Smiling, Elijah rushed over and plopped down.

Laila frowned. "You're not going to eat anything?"

Elijah realized then that he didn't even pick up a plate to eat. He shook his head, "Not hungry. Besides, aren't there more pressing issues at hand?"

"He's right," Rohan chimed in.

Elijah swore he could count every tooth in Rohan's mouth from how wide his smile was.

"We're going on a submarine, y'all! An actual, real-life submarine! And, like, we're going to be, like, doing stuff and, y'know . . ." he shook his hands around, eyes bulging with excitement. "We're going on a goddamn submarine!"

Laila put her palm in front of Rohan's face.

"Thanks for the memo, bud, but we knew that." She put her hand down, then, despite herself, smiled. "But yeah, it is a little surreal, isn't it?"

Elijah nodded. "Tomorrow, no less. I mean, I get that it's a summative project and we're going to have the commanders breathing down our necks the whole time, but still. I probably shouldn't be this excited about something that could cost me my AP status."

The others nodded in agreement. A silence fell upon the group for a moment as they all sat in quiet anticipation.

"So," Rohan said, slightly fidgety, "what'd you guys pack?"

"Forget that," Elijah responded. "Who else is coming with us? I know the Leagues and Lars are, but who else? I couldn't see too much from the back of the room."

"Same," agreed Rohan.

"You guys didn't see Cassidy at the meeting?" Laila asked. Her face crinkled as she frowned.

From the look of disgust on her face, Elijah could tell she wasn't the biggest fan of Cassidy.

"Actually, don't answer. I don't blame you if you did forget. I can't stand that whiney, conceited, entitled little—"

"Who else did you see?" Rohan interrupted.

Laila huffed. "Ten people are embarking, not including the commanders. If we count us, the Leagues, Lars, and Cassidy—"

Elijah noticed the subtle scoff Laila gave when she mentioned Cassidy's name.

"—that means there are three others." She paused, surveying the hall, before letting out a breath of triumph and pointing across the room.

"You see that kid over there?"

Elijah and Rohan followed her finger to a table three rows away. There, surrounded by a couple of friends Elijah knew from AP, sat a white kid with jet black hair that Elijah just couldn't remember the name of. By the look on Rohan's face, he didn't recognize the boy either.

"J–, J–, Jordan?" Rohan said meekly. Immediately afterward, he remarked, "No, that's not right. I've seen him around, for sure, but I don't remember his name."

"Jacob," Laila retorted confidently. "We had a session together a few weeks ago learning how to deal with fire hazards, how to repair a broken vessel, that kind of stuff. He isn't that interesting, to be honest. He just puts his head down and does whatever he's told."

"You do that too, hypocrite," Elijah snorted, jabbing at her with his elbow.

She glared back at him until he was forced to break eye contact.

"Yeah, but I'm actually interesting outside of class. I have a life, hobbies, things I want to pursue outside of the Navy once I graduate. Him?" she said, tilting her head in Jacob's direction. "He strikes me as a boring guy. I don't know why. Maybe it's just intuition."

"That doesn't seem fair," Rohan responded, frowning slightly. "You shouldn't judge someone you hardly know."

"Yeah, well," Laila said exasperated, "we're going to find out soon enough, aren't we? Being packed in a submarine like a bunch of sardines will give us a real taste for each other's character."

Elijah groaned. "Anyone else you recognized and would like to mercilessly categorize?"

"Big words don't make you sound smart, moron," she jabbed back. "And yeah, I do. Peter Maxwell."

Elijah unintentionally let out an agitated huff. He rested his head in his hands as her words set in. Peter was embarking with them. Peter. Of course, there had to be a catch. There was no doubt that Elijah had met his fair share of difficult people at the compound. For one, the commanders seemed more interested in getting their daily power trip than actually helping the recruits. The asshats from his first month harassed him constantly for his complexion. Hell, even Sebastian could be a lot to handle at times. Still, none of these people came anywhere close to the scummy, douchey, insufferable sack of garbage that was Peter. Elijah scowled even thinking of his name.

Peter was the type of kid who would wring a toddler's neck simply for looking at him funny. The first day Elijah got here, it took less than a minute for something in his head to click and tell him that the dude had anger issues. Whenever Elijah saw him, he would either be completely alone with his head hung low, or he would be screaming at anyone that had the stupidity to stand within a ten-foot radius of him. He carried an aura of discomfort and stress wherever he went that could wither flowers and suffocate angels.

To Elijah, Peter just seemed like a kid who was sad all the time and projected it with anger. It was a bold assumption to make considering that Elijah hadn't been around Peter much, but his intuition wouldn't change. Elijah shook his head and looked back at his friends. Laila had a sincere apologetic look on her face while Rohan was cracking his knuckles silently in frustration. With heavy heads, they all turned to look each other in the eyes. One thing was for certain. No matter what that kid's past was or how good of a person he was on the inside, nobody here wanted to be alone on a submarine with him.

"So," Rohan said.

"Yeah."

"That sucks."

"Yeah."

There was silence for a few moments. Then Elijah huffed, "You guys feeling nearly as excited anymore?

Laila scoffed. "Are you insane? An unstable jerk isn't going to dampen my spirits. We're going on a submarine and doing something worthwhile with our AP rank. Keyword: submarine. We're going on a submarine. *A submarine.*" She paused and glanced in Rohan's direction. "Yeah, I get what you mean now."

Rohan smirked. "I'm honestly a bit confused how people like the Leagues, Cassidy, and Peter get to go, though. They said this was supposed to be for the best recruits to prove their rank."

Elijah snapped his fingers and responded.

"The Leagues make sense. Sebastian's not a great guy, and Debra is inches away from a breakdown 24/7, but they work well together and have a knack for technology from what I've heard. So does Lars." Elijah stumbled over his words for a second and sighed. "Yeah, but Cassidy and Peter? Lottery. Had to have been. Kind of a stupid system, huh?"

The other two nodded.

"So that leaves one, then," Rohan calculated. "Well? Spill it, Laila. Guarantee it can't be worse than Peter."

Laila shrugged her shoulders. "I don't remember." She sped up her pace after a disappointing look from both Elijah and Rohan. "Well I mean, I saw him. I just don't recognize him. I can't really put a name to the face."

Rohan grunted in exasperation. "Alright. What then?"

Elijah's stomach grumbled throughout the room, drawing a few stares from other people. He didn't realize how hungry he was until then, and he was beginning to feel like a steamroller was turtling over his stomach inch by inch.

"You know what?" Elijah blurted out. "How about we just eat something?" His stomach growled again, this time bellowing much deeper than before. Elijah clutched the table. "Oh god, let's eat ANYTHING. We'll figure out the other dude when we board tomorrow. Please, somebody just get me some food."

Rohan laughed and whacked Elijah on the back. "Come on, Eli, before you keel over on us."

Rohan and Laila had a good chuckle over that, but Elijah paid no attention to them. All he could think about was the food that—while undercooked, burnt, and barely edible in reality—looked like a buffet fit for a king to his starving self.

Chapter Four

Boarding

Squinting into the darkness, Elijah slipped out of his bunk bed and swung his foot around for proper footing. His ankle caught Rohan's bunk. It was already empty.

He landed silently onto the floor of the room and tip-toed across to the door to the hall, wincing at every creak the frail floor made. He had to be careful not to wake his fellow recruits, as he was awake an hour earlier than normal. Eventually, Elijah made it to the door. Before twisting the doorknob, however, he felt a pang of paranoia strike his heart. Swiftly and noiselessly, Elijah unzipped his bag and reached between a fold of clothes at the bottom. With a swift but subtle jerk, he ruffled the clothes. For a second, a sound like jellybeans in a glass jar reverberated soft enough that only Elijah could hear it. He sighed. The pills were secure. After zipping the bag up and shaking with relief, he slinked out the room and into the hall.

As he traversed the compound, he thought back to the night before. The commanders hadn't given the recruits any instructions for the following day. The only thing CDR Brookes had told them was to get up an hour earlier than usual, or she'd "get on over there and wake everyone else up, too."

Obviously, none of them wanted to be responsible for pissing off a room full of short-tempered buff teenagers, so they listened. The problem was that they didn't have any alarm clocks to get them up in the first place. They always just depended on a commander barging in and screaming at everyone to wake up.

Luckily, Elijah managed to circumvent the little 'waking up on time' problem by simply not sleeping. Like, at all. He was so full of anxiety and energy that he just flopped around in his bunk, staring deep into the darkness in a miserable state of awareness. He yawned as he walked down the hallway. The knowledge that there was likely one person that slept in and was getting a rude awakening cheered him up a bit, and he smiled. Then he yawned again. He was exhausted beyond comprehension, and it likely wasn't a wise use of energy to be feeling anything other than the pure will to keep trudging over to the exit. Thus, he gritted his teeth and kept going.

After what seemed like an eternity, Elijah approached the doors to the outside and threw them open. Instantly, shards of freezing wind penetrated his defenseless skin and sent a prolonged shiver down his spine. Eyes shut tighter than ever, he waddled over to the small building sitting aside the ocean. The inside was illuminated, meaning all the recruits and the commanders were likely already there. Finally, Elijah rested his frozen hand on the doorknob and twisted it open, revealing his dozing crew and high-alert commanders. Rohan, who was sitting closest to the door, winced as Elijah walked in.

"Jesus Christ, Elijah," he sputtered out, "close the damn door! I'm not trying to get hypothermia right before diving a couple thousand feet underwater."

Elijah scoffed. "Believe it or not, you're not the sole person sharing that sentiment, dumbass."

He considered leaving the door ajar just to spite Rohan, but his intense discomfort got the best of him, and he shut the door. He walked over to the chair beside Rohan and plopped down his bag before collapsing down into the seat. He shook his legs like a madman, attempting to heat himself up any way he could. When he looked up, he saw the commanders chatting nonchalantly, wearing fewer layers of clothing than everyone else in the room. He couldn't believe his eyes. What the hell do they do to commanders in "commander-camp" or wherever the hell they come from? They can't be human, standing there in their thin uniforms like it's not unfathomably bitter outside.

Minutes later, more people trickled in, equally numb from the chill outside. Laila came first, hopping up and down rapidly like a rabbit on ketamine. Next was Lars, followed by the Leagues and

Jacob. All but one recruit was present. Minutes passed, and CDR Patrick began pacing back and forth in the room. Elijah couldn't tell why, but when he heard Patrick muttering something about "waking up the whole damn compound if so-and-so doesn't get their butt down here," he got the gist of it.

Just when it seemed like CDR Patrick would actually leave to fetch the last person, that said person burst through the doors and hustled over to the opposite side of the room before throwing his bag at an empty seat. Elijah caught a glimpse of his face as he walked by and realized he was the one that no one could identify at Mess. It took him a second to attach a name to the face, but finally, he realized he was staring at Zachary King.

Discomfort swelled in Elijah's stomach as he looked at Zach. It was hard to articulate but acknowledging Zach's presence just felt wrong to Elijah. It had to be the history that they shared. What else could it be?

Way back when Elijah first got on the bus to the compound, he had a seat to himself and uninterrupted solitude for the four-hour drive. No one spoke to him whatsoever, which was excellent news since it allowed him to catch up on some much-needed shut-eye. Unfortunately, the rough jolty movement of the bus on the gravelly road made it impossible for Elijah to get comfortable. At some point, he opened his eyes in frustration and caught sight of a behemoth of a man staring back at him. Without exaggeration, the dude's biceps were the size of Elijah's legs. They made eye contact for a moment before Elijah turned back and stared at the bus seat in front of him. For the rest of the trip, he couldn't shake the feeling that the man was still staring at him.

Two days later, their paths crossed again. Elijah was waddling back to the dorms, trying to ignore the incredible pain in his legs from running, when Zach entered the hallway on the opposite end. Elijah instantly recognized him as the hulk guy he saw on the bus, and for whatever reason, stopped.

"Hey, I saw you on the bus!" Elijah said.

Zach stopped and smiled slightly. "Yeah, I thought you looked familiar." His voice was surprisingly level for a man that looked like he could snap Elijah like a twig. "My name's Zach." He stretched his hand out for Elijah to shake. He complied.

"Elijah."

"That's a cool name," Zach remarked. "Say, would you want to sit next to me during Mess? I don't really know anyone else here."

"Oh!" Elijah said in surprise. He stammered over his words for a few seconds while considering the offer. From first glance, Zach did seem like an okay guy, but Elijah was already sitting next to Rohan and Laila. He didn't want to give that up to chill with someone he barely knew. He took a breath.

"Sorry, Zach. I kinda have my own crew."

To his surprise, Zach smiled.

"That's alright, bro. I get it. I'll see you around, though."

With that, he punched Elijah on the shoulder and started pounding down the hall.

To Zach's credit, he was correct about seeing Elijah around. Every now and then, when Elijah was swimming laps in the pool, hiking with a fifty-pound backpack weighing him down, or just eating in Mess, Zach would be nearby. For the first couple of weeks, they were pretty close, almost as close as Elijah was with Rohan. When the stress piled on and his other friends were nowhere to be seen, Zach was always there to hang out with. He wasn't the most intelligent person ever—Elijah figured him to be an airhead, actually—but his strength more than made up for it.

They had drifted apart since then, and if Elijah was thinking right, they hadn't spoken in over two months. Since then, things had gotten awkward between the two, and Elijah found it difficult to pretend that things were normal. He always had the support of his other friends, so losing Zach as one didn't bother him much, but the knowledge that Zach had basically zero other acquaintances made Elijah feel guilty, as though he was the sole reason for Zach's solitude. The bleak reality that he would be spending dozens of hours in a cramped space with the man he felt he betrayed finally dawned on him. This was going to be a very long ride.

Elijah turned to his left and raised an eyebrow at Rohan. There was little visibility in the room, but Elijah could just barely make out Rohan raising his eyebrow, too. He had also seen Zach walk in and was likely thinking the same thoughts as Elijah. Ever so slightly, Elijah grinned. Somehow, he and Rohan were always on the same wavelength: the sign of a true friendship.

Out of nowhere, CDR Patrick smashed his hands together and woke the entire room from their momentary slumber. Elijah winced hard and could feel his heart thump faster. He swore that the only reason Patrick ever did that was for the power trip he got from seeing the startled looks on everyone's faces.

"Aight, get on up, now," he thundered. "All ten of you are here on time for once, and it'd be stupid to waste any more time. The submarine's just outside the dock. Brookes will help you board."

He glanced over at Brookes before tilting his head in the direction of the door. She nodded and quickly jogged out of the dock, showering everyone else in the room with piercing cold in the process.

"As we said before, this is one of the smaller submarines, so it shouldn't take more than ten minutes for you to be inside and ready."

Just behind Elijah, someone groaned under their breath before catching themselves. CDR Patrick looked in the direction of the grunt and straightened his shoulders.

"Well, if you're going to be like that, I suppose we can make it twenty minutes. Hell, maybe we can even confiscate your coats beforehand, so you don't have to lug around as much material. Sound good?"

No one said a word.

"That's what I thought. Get out there."

Bit by bit, everyone started to get up and stretch. Elijah swore he heard at least a dozen bone-cracks as people stretched and hopped in place with adrenaline. He, too, was filled to the brim with excitement. After all the wait, he was finally going to set foot in the damn thing. As Rohan described so eloquently, *"We're going in a submarine, man!"*

He twisted his neck around, trying to locate Rohan. Weirdly enough, he wasn't in the room. That's when Elijah caught sight of him sauntering through the door and out into the cold with Laila just behind him. Elijah let out a heavy sigh before walking over to the door with everyone else. With his hands in his pockets, his neck shaking like a madman, and his smile wide as ever, he braved the frost and stomped out onto the dock.

Chapter Five

Descent

Laila whispered, "I'm going to be honest. This is surreal and all, but I kind of hoped this place would be bigger."

Elijah agreed. He and the others entered the hatch of the submarine fifteen minutes ago and had since been tramping around the place. Once they got over the chills from outside, they grew entranced by their surroundings. Besides the fact that they were finally inside of the sub, the technological interior struck all of them by surprise. Tiny computer dashboards, dials, and blinking lights suffocated the walls, and what wasn't plastered with technology was shining brilliantly and metallically in all directions. CDR Brookes noticed everyone's awe.

"Well, what'd you expect?" she laughed. "You thought a submarine would be completely bare on the inside? This is where the real operations get done, kiddos." She glanced over at one of the few empty walls. "Oh, and it's brand-spanking-new, too."

She turned to everyone else and lowered her voice.

"So if I catch one tiny spill, one mess, one *spot,* y'all are gonna face my wrath up on the surface. We're just borrowing this baby from the Coast Guard for this program; we don't actually own the thing. You're setting an example for the curriculum of advanced Navy recruits for years to come." Her grin gradually returned. "So, y'know, no pressure."

"Brookes," CDR Patrick grunted at the front of the submarine, where the major control schematics were. He was fiddling around with a screen with a radar signal on it. "Need some help over here."

She glanced back at the recruits and smiled warmly one last time before darting off toward Patrick. Elijah barely noticed his own subtle smile forming in response. Brookes was easily his favorite commander. To be fair, he rarely saw her, but she was still an awesome person regardless. Elijah remembered the first time he had to climb a twenty-foot rope and ring a bell during his first week at camp. He was fit and able, obviously, but he never practiced anything even remotely similar to rope-climbing. The movements and rhythm needed to complete the test were beyond him. While everyone else's success echoed in screams of jubilation throughout the gym, he still struggled with taking his feet off the ground. He undoubtedly would've failed if it wasn't for Brookes' coaching and patience. It took well over four times as long as everyone else, but eventually, Elijah's finger just barely managed to swipe the bell and secure his spot in AP. Just thinking about what would have happened that day had CDR Patrick been stationed made Elijah shiver. To him, Patrick could learn a thing or two from Brookes' tough-love methods.

Elijah snapped out of his daze and caught sight of everyone wandering to look around the sub. He sped over to Rohan's side and was about to start talking before something slammed into his left shin. It took less than a second for waves of blinding pain to begin overwhelming him.

"Jesus, bro," Rohan muttered, backing away from Elijah's pained expression. "What the hell's the matter with you?"

Elijah furrowed his brow and hissed through clenched teeth until the pain finally started to taper off. Then, still squinting and grasping his leg in shock, he turned towards the object that caused him so much agony. There was a small metal box with a few switches and a half-dozen blinking lights on it that jutted out from the wall in an elusive way. Elijah had just struck it with his shinbone with the power of a semi-truck.

By this time, Rohan had transitioned from genuine concern to fits of laughter.

"Oh my god," he wheezed between gasps for air, "the one time you look like a complete moron, it isn't even because of me!" He paused. "Wait. Is that good or bad?"

"Shut the hell up," Elijah groaned, which only made Rohan chortle harder. Furious, Elijah kicked the box with his unharmed foot. The box made a strange whirring sound before going back to normal. "Why the hell is everything here so jam-packed anyway?" Elijah questioned. "Either you're breathing someone else's air, or you almost kill yourself just trying to traverse the damn place."

"It's a submarine, idiot," Cassidy jabbed, walking in on the two from behind. Her voice was gravelly and uninterested, somehow even more than usual. "The whole point of the thing is to be compact and light while fitting as much tech as possible. Do you really think they're gonna change the whole design of a war machine so that people like you don't hit a six-inch box on the side of the wall?"

"Hey, Cassidy," Rohan muttered, eyes shifted downward. "Nice to see you, too."

Cassidy rolled her eyes. Elijah could feel his muscles tightening up. He had never talked to Cassidy face-to-face before, and he was only now beginning to realize how lucky he was for that to be the case. It was unbelievable how unlikable she was. All that he knew about her was that all the commanders despised her and that she was only in AP because she was the best swimmer stationed. That, by itself, should've given him the indication that she wasn't a very fun person to hang around. And yet, hearing her talk with such vitriol and acidity made him want to throw up. Great. Patrick, Zach, Peter and Cassidy. You could make a barbershop quartet out of these clowns, and that still wouldn't make tolerating them any easier.

"You good, dude?" Cassidy waved her hand in front of Elijah's face. "I'm pretty sure you hit your leg on that thing, not your head."

Elijah pushed her arm away. "Yeah. I'm jolly. Thanks." He took a deep breath. *Jolly? Really?* "So, where is everyone else?"

"What do you think, moron?" she spit. "We're looking around the place and seeing where we'll be sleeping for the next few days."

Before Elijah could respond, Rohan grabbed his arm and started pacing down the hall, away from Cassidy and her snobbish comments. Elijah could feel his blood boiling.

She would get along just fine with Peter, he thought. A match made in hell.

A minute later, Rohan had dragged Elijah over to the quarters, where Laila, Jacob, and Debra were at. It was an odd feeling, being able to get from one side of the place to the other in just a few steps. He was so used to dashing through a massive compound every day that walking across a mini-sub in three minutes put him off. He followed Rohan into the room and caught sight of Laila fixing the sheets on her bunk. He waved, and she smiled and waved back.

"Where've you two been?" she asked, struggling to fix one end of her bedsheets under her mattress.

Rohan sighed. "Don't even ask." He looked over and around at the bunks surrounding them. "So, do we just pick a place or what?"

Laila shook her head. "Nope. There's a paper tag taped to the side of every bed. You just have to look closely, but it's there."

With that information, the two friends split up to find their respective bunk. Elijah stared intensely into the wood of every bunk in the room before coming to the realization that he was staring at absolutely nothing. If there were tags on the sides of every bunk, wouldn't they be visible from a distance? He was about to ask Laila what she was talking about when Rohan interrupted his thoughts.

"Jesus, it's like a prison cell in here," he observed, gliding his hands across all of the beds. "Five beds on one side, five on another, all completely white with garbage mattresses." His eyes widened for a moment. "Oh my god. Is this what I signed up for?"

"Are you kidding me?" retorted Laila, with a disbelieving look on her face. "Everything you've gone through in training, everything you've had to do as an AP, and you draw the line at suboptimal mattresses?"

There was a pause as Rohan pouted and stared at the floor in embarrassment. "I take my sleep seriously."

Laila groaned and covered her face with her hands. "I don't believe you people." She looked back up and noticed that the two were still searching for their beds. "What are you still doing? Just find the tag, dummies."

"Yeah, little problem there," Elijah grunted, giving up on his search. "There's no goddamn tags anywhere."

"Really?" Laila responded. She looked genuinely puzzled.

"That's because they all wore off," came a voice from behind.

Everyone turned, startled. Jacob Campbell was lying in his own bed, eyes shut, but it was evident that he was the one who had spoken.

"They've been planning this thing for a long time, so they probably put the tags up months ago. Laila must've been the latest one on the roster, so hers hasn't worn off in that time." He opened his eyes and cleared his throat, drowsily looking at Elijah. "If you want to find your bunk, glide your hand under the bottom of the bed. Check to see if that's your bag. If it is: bingo. That's what I did, at least."

"Hey, thanks Jacob," Rohan said, beaming. "That's really helpful of you."

Jacob shrugged. "If it gets you people to settle down faster, I'm all for it."

Elijah decided to follow Jacob's method and got down on his knees to feel under the bed. He hit a bag after a second and pulled it out, revealing a brown bag with a worn sticker of a computer with a smiley face and off-center military beret. The computer was saluting with a USB cord that was plugged into its side, and underneath it all was text that read "Compute and Salute" in green ASCII-style font.

Elijah heard rustling from behind and turned around to see Debra staring at the bag. Before he could even blink, she had already hopped off of her bed and towered over him.

"That belongs to my brother," she stuttered, pointing a quivering finger at the bag. "I think that your bed might be somewhere else."

Slowly, Elijah got up and backed away from her and the bag.

"Alright," he said, hands up in a defensive position. "I'll go find my own."

He swore that Debra continued to stare at him without blinking as he walked around her. To be fair, he knew that the Leagues were both strange in their own individual ways. He knew that Debra always acted hyper and alien for no reason, and Sebastian was, well, Sebastian. Yet, he was still constantly caught off guard every time he made contact with her. He never seemed to be able to digest her bizarre nature like everyone else.

Welp, weird is better than instigating, he reasoned. He'd take Debra to be a companion over Peter or Cassidy any day.

This time, when Elijah swung his leg under the bed, he caught a familiar material. He pulled it out and investigated the zippers, dark green color, and familiar food stains. After a minute, he could confirm that the bag was his. After checking to make sure everyone was preoccupied, he swiftly shook his clothes at the bottom between his two hands. Pills clattered around the hidden bottle, and Elijah winced slightly. The noise was louder than he had anticipated. He turned around again to make sure nobody had heard and sure enough, nobody seemed to notice. Jacob was still relaxing on his bed, Debra was staring attentively at the ceiling, and Rohan was yanking at his own bag, which was jammed underneath a bunk. The only person that heard was Laila, just five feet away, who glanced at him and raised an eyebrow. Elijah just shrugged his shoulders and zipped his bag up again before slamming himself onto his frail mattress.

Elijah could trust Laila with anything, and that included his insomnia meds. Rohan was a great friend and all, without a doubt, but he had known Laila forever. She was his ride-or-die and had been for years. Elijah closed his eyes and allowed himself to sink deeper and deeper into the warmth and comfort that his mattress provided for him. He definitely had a couple of lunatics with him, but the fact that she and Rohan would be there with him made him feel a tiny bit better.

Gradually, more and more people began trickling in. Elijah kept his eyes closed and eavesdropped on their conversations. He heard Peter cursing every vulgarity in the dictionary while attempting to find his bunk before Jacob helped him out. He heard Debra and Sebastian talk once he came in and got settled. Finally, he heard the room hush when Zach sliced through and collapsed into his bed, causing the bed to creak with the stress of holding up all his weight. After around a half-hour, the room was still.

Minutes later, the silence was interrupted by a deep humming that subtly shook the room and everybody inside. Elijah could make out footsteps coming down the hallway from the front of the submarine and realized he had only a few seconds until it was lights out, and he wouldn't be able to see a thing. He haphazardly flipped over his bed, dangling on by a thread, and dug through his bag. He could make out Zach and the Leagues staring at him in bewilderment, but he didn't care. Shoving his hand deeper in, he finally grasped the pills and clutched them out. At that moment, the lights in the room shut off.

Under the cover of darkness, he zipped his bag up, elbowed it beneath his bed, and flung himself back over into bed. Even though there were no lights on in the room, he could tell his face was turning bright red. It didn't matter to him. Without those pills, he wasn't getting an hour of sleep.

"Hey, buddy," a voice called out.

Elijah turned over to see Zach's glowing gray eyes staring at him back in the darkness. "You doing alright?"

Elijah nodded before realizing that what he was doing was barely visible. He cleared his throat and answered, "Yeah, uh, just forgot to, um, y'know, get my sleeping mask. Blindfold. That I sleep with." If there was no one else in the room, he would've screamed into his pillow from frustration at himself.

Zach was silent for a moment.

"Where'd you get a sleeping mask from?"

Elijah felt a bead of sweat trickle down his neck.

"Oh, well . . . you know, from . . . well, you know."

More silence.

"No. I don't know."

At that moment, the footsteps were ringing just outside the dorm doors, and Elijah finally had an excuse to stop talking. He closed his eyes, sighing from relief before wiping the sweat off his neck. Three seconds later, the commanders barged inside. It was difficult to see in the darkness, but Elijah thought that CDR Patrick actually looked somewhat stirred and animated, which differed dramatically from his usual stiff self. Elijah guessed it was because the project was actually getting underway after all this time. Days, possibly weeks of anticipation, and it was finally going to happen.

CDR Brookes approached from behind him and began knocking on the metal outline of the hull, causing an echoing noise that caught everyone's attention.

"Alright, everybody. This is it. It's currently . . ." she paused and checked her watch, "5:40 a.m. I know this is around the time y'all would be getting up but consider this an act of mercy. We'll let you catch some more sleep while the submarine heads down to the point where we can start the assignment. No horseplay. No jokes. No nothing. We don't want to end this thing before we even start it."

She scanned around the room.

"Glad we're on the same page. See y'all in three to four hours."

She flicked CDR Patrick on the shoulder and started pacing out the room again before she stopped in her tracks.

"Oh!" she yelled suddenly, turning as she spoke. "If anyone needs us, which you probably won't, we'll be in two separate rooms near the control room. If any of you see a leak or something dangerous, just come running out screaming and find us. This is the safest submarine we got, but still." She motioned around the room. "See something, say something. It's only four hours. You'll survive."

With that, CDR Patrick smacked a button on the wall that ended the incessant humming in the walls. The newfound silence was broken only by his and Brookes' fading footsteps, leaving everyone else in complete sensory deprivation.

Elijah sighed and tossed over in his bed. He pulled out the pill bottle and quietly took the cap off, tossing two pills into his hand. He paused for a moment, debating with himself, then put one back. If he was only sleeping for four hours, a single pill would be perfectly fine for him. Grimacing, he placed the pill on his tongue and dry swallowed it, gripping his neck and trying desperately not to cough and disrupt the quietness.

He could already feel the effects beginning to take place. The world swirled above him, and he felt his arms and legs fall under a wonderful sort of paralysis as they began to rest. A smile forming slowly across his face, he took a deep breath and stuffed the pills back under his pillow. He closed his eyes and curled up in his blanket as the world around him slowly melted away. He sunk deeper into the mattress as he drifted off into dreamless sleep.

CHAPTER SIX

CASUALTIES

Pop.

That was the first sound that flushed Elijah's ears when he opened his groggy eyes hours later. Groaning, he turned his head around and slowly rustled the sheets off of himself. The pops reverberated throughout his head, similar to the sensation of ascending to the sky in an airplane. After a moment, they subsided, which was good: it allowed him to better hear the blood-curdling screeches of his companions down the hall.

Elijah had woken up to chaos just once before. When he was about seven, a fire had broken out in the boiler room of the basement in his home back in New Mexico. With everyone ignorant, it began crawling up the wooden house, licking the walls with its furious flames and filling his home with dreadful gray smoke. He awoke to his father, a calm, collected, generally sane man, frantically screaming at Elijah to get out of bed and run downstairs out of the house, coughing as he spoke and inhaled the thickening smoke. His screams were deafened by the sounds of active smoke alarms, but Elijah still remembered his tone. Wild. Panicked, even. It was horrible. But it was nothing, absolutely nothing compared to what Elijah was hearing right now.

Before he knew it, Elijah was out of bed and dragging himself out of the room, towards the screams and terror. He felt disconnected as he walked, as though he were in a dream. He floated forward, grabbing boxes and beams as he walked to support his shaking knees. While fear hadn't fully infiltrated his mind yet, his body already knew something was wrong. The screams increased in volume as he walked, until he finally walked into the engine area and caught sight of Debra, who was on the floor, face-up, eyes flowing with tears. Her jaw was shuttering as silent sobs croaked out of her body. She whipped her face around to meet Elijah, who by this time was fully aware of his surroundings. He didn't get a chance to ask a question before she began to speak.

"They're . . . she's just . . . I don't even know how anyone . . ." she sputtered incoherently.

Elijah stared at her blankly for a moment before turning to his left, where Laila, Rohan, and Sebastian were standing around, eyes wide with shock, not acknowledging Elijah's presence whatsoever. Finally, Elijah had enough. The pressure was becoming overwhelming.

"Guys . . ." he whispered, causing everyone in the room to flick their heads around to face him. He took a breath and composed himself. "What the hell is going on?"

None of them moved a muscle, except Sebastian, whose chest was heaving breath after breath. Then, Rohan lifted his shaking hand and pointed in front of the trio.

Elijah felt a painful sensation in his gut as he approached. Laila and Sebastian shuffled to the side, allowing Elijah a full view of the source of the chaos, the cause of the terror. He took a step back, wheezing what little air his lungs could manage.

CDR Brookes and CDR Patrick were dead.

Well, Elijah couldn't see their faces on account of them being face down on the floor, but he recognized the uniforms immediately. Deep crimson blood replaced the soft beige of Patrick's left breast pocket. Elijah suspicions were confirmed when he peered closer. It was a bullet hole. He didn't get a chance to look at Brookes before his body gave up, and he fell to the ground. His ears started ringing again, so he put his hands up to try to block the sound. Thousands of thoughts raced through his mind, and not a single one was articulable. For a moment, just a moment, Elijah was in the purest form of confusion and disarray that he had ever experienced. It was maddening.

He opened his eyes to his friends, all of whom were mirroring the emotions he was feeling as well. Rohan was staring at the ceiling, rocking back and forth on his butt like a toddler. Sebastian had his head tucked between his knees, and Laila was staring at Elijah with the exact same expression as before. Apart from Debra's frantic sobbing, there was silence in the room. After what felt like an eternity, Laila finally stood up and looked around at everyone.

"Wow," she muttered. Then, to everyone's surprise, she chuckled. Just once. It almost could've been mistaken for a hiccup, or a sob. But it was a chuckle. There was no doubt about it. "This isn't happening."

Elijah rested his face in his hands before pulling them back in surprise. They were wet. He had been crying, and he hadn't even realized. He closed his eyes again and, using his elbow to prop himself up, stood.

"We need to get everyone back into the quarters," he coughed. "We should probably leave the . . ." he paused and cleared his throat. ". . . leave the bodies where they're at until then."

Rohan stopped rocking and looked up at Elijah with a puzzled expression.

"Wait," he frowned. "They said they would be sleeping in the rooms on the opposite side of the control room right before lights out. How'd they end up here?"

Out of nowhere, Debra inhaled so roughly that it sounded like she had been drowning for the past five minutes. The four turned around and stared at her.

"Peter . . ." she began before pausing for a moment. "Peter . . . he found them with the rest of us and . . . he just . . ." her eyes glazed over. "He just picked them up. Like it was nothing. Said something about keeping them together in one room. Then he brought them over to the control room and dropped . . ." her voice caught on the last word, and she returned to staring intently at the ground.

"He picked them up from the side rooms and just plopped them here?" Rohan asked.

His face probably should've been concerned, but the only emotion Elijah could find was one of sullenness.

Debra nodded.

"Okay," Laila said, clapping her hands together. "Elijah is right. We need to get everyone together in the quarters right now." She snuck a glance at the corpses of her former mentors and shuddered. "And for the love of God, somebody find Peter."

Sebastian laughed after Laila finished speaking, prompting everyone to look at him. His laughter transformed into hiccups until he finally looked at Laila and clicked his tongue.

"You must be out of your goddamn mind, Laila." He put his hand up to silence her before she could rebuttal. "Just wait. Just listen. If I'm hearing you correctly," he said as his voice grew deeper, "you want us to split up, run around the sub searching for everybody, all while there's a murderer on the loose? You understand that, right?" His hands began to shake. "You understand that this is literally the single worst opportunity to split up and search for a MURDERER!"

"Stop," Debra wailed from her seat near the hallway. "Stop it, Sebastian."

Everyone ignored her.

Laila rested her chin on her palm and thought.

"Y'know what, Sebastian?" she questioned. "You're right. You're actually right for once. That's a stupid idea. We'll partner up." She turned to Debra and snapped her fingers twice. "Debra. Hey. Debra, get up."

Debra lifted herself up and walked over to the group while hugging her arms around herself. She was still shaking, albeit not as much as before.

Laila pointed at Sebastian next. "You two will go together. Only makes sense for siblings to stick together. Just walk around and tell everyone to meet at the quarters." When they didn't move, she raised her voice. "Go. Now."

Finally, Sebastian pulled Debra's arm over his shoulder and lifted her up. Everyone watched him guide her out of the room until they disappeared behind the wall. When their footsteps began to fade, Laila turned back around to face Elijah and Rohan.

"We need someone to stay here with the bodies," she said matter-of-factly. "Who'll it be?"

"Now just hold on a second," Rohan interjected. "You want somebody to stay here alone to guard a bunch of dead bodies?" He gagged and brought his hand up to his mouth. "Oh my god. That was a sentence I never thought I'd have to say."

"Until we get everyone in the quarters, somebody has to guard them. We can't have somebody be like Peter and just pick them up and move them around. Besides, they're beginning to smell horrible. The sooner we have everyone in one room, the faster we can . . . uh . . . dispose of them."

Rohan shook his head. "The world's gone mad."

Laila grunted. "Yeah. If it bothers you two so much, I can stay here while you two search for the stragglers."

Something about letting Laila sit alone with the decomposing bodies of the commanders didn't sit right with Elijah, but he knew what the alternative was. It was at a moment like this that he should've interrupted and declared courageously that he would be the one to guard the bodies and brave the solitude. Frankly, though, he was under a combination of intense distress, emotional exhaustion, and the after-effects of the pills he took last night. He was in no condition to guard them or anything else, for that matter.

"Rohan," Elijah said. "Come on. Let's go."

Rohan furrowed his brow. "We're just gonna leave Laila here by herself?"

"I can handle myself just fine, thanks," Laila countered.

"You're gonna be hanging out alone in a cramped control room with the corpses of mentors you've known for months while there's a high chance of a murderer roaming around the submarine we're on." Rohan shrugged his shoulders. "But yeah. If you can handle it, knock yourself out."

Elijah grabbed Rohan's arm and tugged him out of the room with a bit more force than necessary. Once they were back out into the hall, he turned and glared at Rohan. Rohan looked back with a blank expression.

"What?" he said. "Was I wrong?"

Elijah groaned. "Dude, I don't know if you've processed it or not by now, but we are screwed beyond comprehension. This is not the time to be an ass to people we can trust."

The expression on Rohan's face soured.

"People we can trust, huh? Man, twenty-four hours ago we were all talking about how fun it would be to get on the sub and fix radios and crap—and now Patrick and Brookes are dead." He shut his eyes and rubbed them with his index fingers. "It's been less than four hours, and the only leaders we have here are dead. If whoever killed them doesn't kill us soon, we'll drown or asphyxiate anyway.

We're . . ." he rolled his eyes to the ceiling and took a breath. "We're gonna die, Elijah."

"Now just hold on a second," Elijah said, trying to ignore the last thing Rohan said. "We don't know for sure that these were murders."

Rohan raised an eyebrow.

"You can't be serious. You saw the same bodies I did, bro. Explain to me how two commanders mysteriously die of bullet wounds to the back in a secure submarine where the only other people are recruits. One of us took them out."

Suddenly, Rohan shut his eyes and slammed his fist into the wall, prompting a metallic groan from the area he hit. He exhaled heavily and shook his hand limply, muttering under his breath. Then he looked back at Elijah with a dismal expression.

"Face it. There's a killer on the loose."

"There was no sound, though," Elijah countered. "Nobody in the night heard anything, especially not a gunshot. In a place like this, that would wake up the entire crew in a nanosecond."

Rohan shrugged and didn't say anything. For some reason, Elijah disliked the silence more than he did arguing with Rohan. A few seconds later, Rohan waved his hand and started walking down the hall. With an unhidden twinge of hopelessness in his voice, he called out to Elijah, "Let's just go. Better than waiting around."

As much as Elijah hated to admit it, Rohan was right. Reluctantly, he followed Rohan through the cramped hallway while trying unsuccessfully to evict the scent of rotting flesh from his nose. Barely a minute later, they were already back at the quarters. A quick glance around determined that they weren't the only ones. There was a rustling sound in a bed to the left. Elijah turned to see a red-eyed Jacob staring directly back at him.

"I'm guessing you saw," Jacob croaked.

"Yeah," Elijah responded.

Jacob shrugged his shoulders. "Oh well. Not much else to say, is there?" He turned back around in his bed, but not before Elijah caught a glimpse of his tear-stained cheek. He didn't move after that.

"Come on," Rohan called as he tugged on Elijah's sleeve. Elijah turned and saw Lars laying down and reading a book. The light wasn't reaching his face all too well, so Elijah couldn't see his expression. As he approached, he swore that the lights must've been playing tricks on him. Lars looked . . . calm?

He stood there awkwardly, just a foot or two away from Lars without saying anything. For a minute, he completely ignored Elijah and kept reading with the same blank expression on his face. After what seemed like an hour, Lars sighed and put the book down. His eyes moved to meet Elijah's.

"What?" he said. His voice sounded the same as usual.

"Nothing," Elijah responded. He paused. "What're you doing?"

He knew it was a stupid question, and from the look on Lars' face, he knew it, too.

"I'm reading a book," he said. "Catcher in the Rye. I've read it, like, six times since I've been recruited."

Elijah couldn't take it anymore.

"How are you so nonchalant when you know somebody's been murdered?"

Lars smiled. It wasn't a warm smile, but it wasn't cold, either. It felt artificial, like he was being puppeteered around.

"I'm not calm, Elijah. I'm freaking out, and I have no idea what to do with myself. There are a thousand things I want to do, but the only thing I can find the strength to do is sit here and wait."

"For what?" Elijah asked.

He didn't answer.

Elijah pressed on. "Well, at least make yourself useful somehow. You can find a way."

Lars shook his head.

"There's a solid chance the radio in the control room is beyond my ability to fix. Even if I had Sebastian by my side, there's no telling if we'll be dead by the time the signal goes out. Now . . . " he said as he glanced at Elijah, "can you take the hint and leave? I'm busy."

At that moment, Rohan called out to Elijah near his bunk at the end of the room. The quarters were barely big enough to fit the cramped beds, let alone the people that slept on them. To be honest, Elijah could hear a whisper across the room, so there was no reason for Rohan to call out that loudly. Maybe it was just nerves, which Elijah could understand; things were pretty chaotic, after all.

He walked over to Rohan and raised his eyebrows.

"So?" he questioned. "What is it?"

"Pipe down, would you?" Rohan hissed back. Elijah didn't miss the irony in that statement. "I just got done talking to Cassidy. She's almost worse than Debra. Hasn't left her bed since this all began."

A glance over Rohan's shoulder confirmed his statement. Cassidy was rocking back and forth on her bed with her hands on her face, shaking ever so slightly while her jaw quivered in place. The sight was a far cry from the jerk Elijah met last night . . . she looked uniquely vulnerable here. Human.

"Yeah, I can see that," Elijah said. "I don't blame her, honestly. We should all be way more panicked than we are right now."

"Right?" Rohan agreed. "Do you see Lars over there? Man's reading a book like it's a normal off-day on the surface. How can he possibly be so calm after knowing we're in such deep sh—"

"He's not," Elijah interrupted. "I guess that's just how he copes?"

Rohan huffed. "Well, it's putting me off, I'll tell you that much. I'd say we keep an eye on him."

At that moment, there were a series of noises just outside the quarters that began growing in volume. Everyone whipped their heads around and stared, unable to move. Even Lars put his book down and looked at the entrance. The rapid thudding continued for an unsettlingly long time until it suddenly stopped as a shadow emerged from the corner of the doorway. Then two. Finally, the people projecting the shadows showed their faces, and everyone took a sigh of relief.

"We're here," groaned Sebastian, still half-carrying Debra on his back. Three steps into the room, he flung her arm off of his shoulder and plopped her onto the bed next to Jacob who stirred in surprise. Before anyone could ask a question, Sebastian flopped onto the empty bed adjacent to Jacob's and spoke.

"Didn't find anybody," he gasped. "Granted, we barely searched around. We just looked at the rest area and the halls leading from there to here." He nodded in his sister's direction. "She didn't feel safe, so we came back directly after."

Elijah repressed the urge to question whether Debra was the one who felt unsafe.

"Did you see Laila anywhere?"

He shook his head. "As far as I know, she's still with the bodies."

"What about Peter?" Lars asked. "Zach and he are the only ones missing right now if I'm not mistaken."

Sebastian paused.

"Were you reading just now? In the middle of all of this?"

When Lars didn't reply, he responded.

"No, we haven't seen them. Now if you'll excuse me," he said as he tapped Debra on the shoulder, "We're going to bed. Debra and I are not leaving this room until everybody is back inside."

"Well," Cassidy interjected, "how are we supposed to get everybody back inside if we're all in here? Somebody has to look for them. They could be dead already!"

On the other side of the room, Jacob chuckled. "Since when did you get so empathic, Cassidy? As far as I remember, you've only ever cared about yourself."

"This isn't FUNNY!" Cassidy shrieked.

Everyone in the room stopped to look at her. If there was any hint of calm in the room before, it evaporated with that explosion. Cassidy's face grew redder and redder, and she looked like she was on the verge of hyperventilating.

"Brookes—sorry—CDR Brookes and CDR Patrick are dead. We're stuck in a submarine with each other, and the only leaders we have are lying in a pool of their own blood in the engine room. There's only seven of us now. If the other three aren't back yet, we might as well assume that they're dead."

At that moment, the same noise the League siblings made rebounded. Everyone's head turned from Cassidy to the doorway in anticipation. Elijah hadn't realized how much he was panicking about Laila's safety until now, so he was anxious to see who walked in, hoping it was her. Instead, he was greeted with a different face.

"What's up," Peter mumbled as he waltzed into the room, head cast towards the floor.

There was silence for a moment until Jacob scoffed.

"Oh, joy. Peter's here."

"What'd you say?" Peter retorted calmly, turning to face Jacob's bunk.

Jacob's eyes widened.

"Ahh, oh, nothing! Nothing," he sputtered out, forcing himself to sit upright.

He stared at Peter for an uncomfortably long time until Peter continued on down the room. The silence was so thick, Elijah could practically drown in it. Still, despite the uneasiness that he was in, he had to know where Laila was. The thoughts that raced through his mind were too much to bear, and he opened his mouth to ask Peter the question. However, just as he did, the silence was broken by another pair of footsteps. This time, only Elijah, Rohan, and Sebastian bothered to look at the door. Moments later, two people materialized in the doorway.

"Laila!" Elijah cried out.

He cupped his hands over his mouth the instant he spoke, but he couldn't help it. The relief he felt knowing that she was safe washed over him like a tidal wave.

"Hey, Elijah," she replied.

She looked puzzled yet humored at his outburst. Her eyes drifted from him to Rohan, then Debra, then around the room as she counted off everyone with her fingers. She frowned and then counted again before sighing.

"Well, that's everyone. It looks like all ten of us are together."

"Hang on," Lars countered. He counted off the heads in the room on his own. "There's only nine people in here. Where's Zach?"

At the moment, the shadow that was lurking behind Laila revealed itself to be the final person. Zach waltzed into the room and stood by Laila's side, scanning the room and the surprised faces of everyone inside. When his eyes fell upon Elijah's, Elijah felt every molecule of his body shiver with uneasiness. Obviously, there were much more pressing matters at hand, but there was still something instinctively awful about meeting an old friend you don't talk to anymore that makes you want to curl into a ball and hide.

Zach cleared his throat. "Hey guys," he said. His voice was mellower than usual. It missed that energy that Elijah heard whenever they used to joke around together. "Laila and I were guarding CDR Patrick and Brookes over at the control room."

"He found me there all by myself and offered to stay by my side," Laila elaborated. "I said yes, and we both sat on opposite ends of the room making sure nobody went in or out the entrances. When nobody came back to tell us everyone was accounted for, we got worried and headed back."

Her eyes met Elijah's as she said the last part. There wasn't a direct agreement that Elijah had to come get her once everyone was accounted for, but she was still expecting him to show anyway. Elijah diverted his gaze shamefully.

A squeak echoed around the room, and almost everyone turned to look for the rodent that produced the sound. After a moment, they realized the noise came from Cassidy trying to put words together. She cleared her throat and tried again. "Erh, I mean, wha . . . where are the bodies now?"

Zach raised an eyebrow. "Where we left them. Where else?"

Cassidy's eyes bore into the ground.

"Well, I mean, it must've been hard to guard with the bodies on opposite sides of the room, I guess." She paused. "Forget it. It's stupid."

Zach's puzzled expression deepened.

"What are you talking about? They were on top of each other like a pile of laundry."

Suddenly, something clicked in Elijah's mind.

"WAIT!" he blurted out. "Debra told me this earlier. Peter . . . god, what did Peter do?"

All eyes were on Debra now. She wiped her nose with her sleeve and stuttered, "He . . . like, he picked them up, but not before . . . what I meant to say . . ."

"He picked them up like ragdolls and plopped them in the center of the room," Sebastian completed.

He got up and moved over to his sister's bed and put his arm around her, rubbing her shoulder as more sobs escaped her.

The tension after Sebastian said that was inarticulable. Everyone's gaze lasered in on Peter, who was still standing and leaning against the wall opposite of everyone, barely paying attention. When he noticed that the spotlight had shifted to him, he sighed and stared back at everyone else.

After a minute that felt like an eternity, Lars spoke up. "So," he started. "Why?"

Peter frowned. "Why what?"

Lars heaved a sigh and rubbed his temples. "Why did you move the bodies?'

Peter looked away. "I dunno."

Lars kept staring at Peter in disbelief before covering his entire face with his palm.

"Peter," he tried again. "Peter, Peter, Peter. Do you understand how you sound right now?"

"Not really, no."

"We're on a submarine with two dead commanders that weren't dead before. They have bullet wounds that couldn't possibly have been self-inflicted. Therefore, someone here is a murderer. Do you understand how you saying 'oh, I just moved them closer because why not,' might give us an indication that you were the one that pulled the trigger?"

Peter clenched his teeth.

"First of all, Debra was there first. She saw me walk in and find the commanders in that state. If anyone should be suspected, it should be her."

Sebastian stopped comforting Debra and stared at Peter in disbelief.

"Do you actually think that she," he said while motioning at his distressed sister, "could possibly kill somebody?"

Peter shrugged. "I don't know, man. All I know is that Debra was there before I was. And for your information, I didn't toss the bodies around like they were nothing. I dragged them over on top of each other so that they would stay in one place."

This time, Elijah interrogated Peter. "That doesn't make any sense. They were in the same room, just ten feet or so apart. Why would you even think of touching them?"

"It just felt like the right thing to do, okay? I was in shock. I don't even want to think of touching them anymore. I'm not even sure how I did."

"None of what you're saying makes any sense," Rohan said. "Only a murderer would be messing around with bodies after finding them."

It was a subtle movement, but Elijah caught Peter's fists clenching. His voice was shaking at this point, but still maintained the gruffness he always had. "I. Am not. A murderer."

"This conversation isn't going anywhere," Laila announced. She walked forward and took a seat on an empty bed at the center of the commotion. "There's no way we're going to find out who the killer is today."

"Are you kidding?" Jacob scoffed. "Bag search. Everyone here. Right now. The commanders were literally shot dead with a gun. That's not something that's particularly easy to hide."

"I side with Jacob, actually," Elijah apprehensively stated. "The murders are still fresh. Everyone's in one room. It makes the most sense to search everyone and look for clues."

"You idiots," Lars groaned. "There's a radio on the damn submarine. Sebastian and Debra and I can fix it and call for help from the surface instead of playing detective like y'all are doing."

"Wait," Sebastian countered. "Who the hell said I was going anywhere?"

"What, you don't trust me?" Lars spat.

"And what if I don't?"

The room had descended back into commotion. Lars and the Leagues were fighting over their supposed trustworthiness, Jacob and Laila were going at it over what course of action to take, Peter had taken the opportunity to try and steal Rohan's bunk, and Cassidy was screaming into her pillow unintelligibly. Elijah felt his head pound and pound as the voices rose higher and higher and grew thick with vitriol and spite. Just when it seemed like the submarine would snap in half, Zach snatched a metal rod from underneath his bunk and started slamming it against the wall of the room. The screeching echoes pierced through everyone's eardrums and finally got everyone to shut up. A panting Zach dropped the rod and turned to face the bunks, now occupied with slack-jawed men and women.

"Here's what we're going to do," he gasped. He wiped his forehead with his left arm and pointed at the door with his right. "No one leaves this goddamn room. Not tonight. We'll see if anyone can leave in the morning, but tonight, we shelter in place."

A dissenting whisper rang out from the back of the room.

"What was that?" Zach questioned.

Peter cleared his throat, revealing himself to be the dissenting voice. "I said that's insane. I'm not going to stay in a room full of people when I can guarantee one of them is a murderer."

"I second that," Rohan said, though he spoke with significantly less confidence.

"Think of it this way," Zach explained as he began pacing around the room like a passionate professor. "We already know this guy—"

"Or girl!" Rohan interjected. Zach ignored him.

"We already know this guy had an opportunity to kill all of us. The commanders had to be killed when we were sleeping, or we would have heard the gunshots ring out. Maybe whatever feud this killer had was only with them?"

There was silence as everyone pondered his words. While something deep within Elijah's gut felt uneasy about sleeping with everyone else, he couldn't think of any other alternative. Reluctantly, he let his silence communicate his agreement. To varying degrees, everyone else did the same.

"Good," Zach said. "Then it's decided. We sleep here."

"Who made you the boss?" Peter finally challenged. "Ever since you walked in that doorway you've been acting like Patrick."

Zach shrugged. "No one's challenged me yet. Would you want to be the first?"

Peter said nothing, though his expression communicated visible hate. Zach smiled and walked over to the only available bunk before plopping himself down on it.

"Lights out, I guess."

Elijah sighed and turned over in his bunk to grab the underside of his pillow. He ruffled around it for a moment before grabbing the pills he needed and stealthily retrieved them. Just to make sure, he confirmed that everyone was completely lost in their own thoughts before swiping them into view. Confident, he looked up to see Laila staring right back at him. He offered her a small smile. It just seemed like the right thing to do, although he felt stupid immediately afterward. She feebly attempted to mirror his expression before turning around and facing the wall.

Elijah popped the pills into his mouth and swallowed hard before placing the pill bottle back underneath his pillow. He expected them to calm his mind and allow him a restful sleep, but instead all it did was paralyze him as his thoughts echoed in his brain like a scream in an open cavern. Eventually, he lost the strength to keep his eyes open, and he allowed the blankets to carry him away from the burdens of reality, if only for a few hours.

Maybe things would be okay in the morning.

CHAPTER SEVEN

SEARCH AND RESCUE

There was no chaos when Elijah awoke this time. Funnily enough, there was no light, either. He turned over in his bed and squinted deeply in the darkness, trying to lock his eyes onto the clock he knew was right above Laila's bunk. The hands cast uncertain shadows in the inky darkness, but Elijah could still see that it said 9:20. Whether it was a.m. or p.m., he had no idea.

Understanding that there was no way he was going back to sleep, he rolled out of bed and pondered when the lights turned off, since he never remembered them doing so automatically. He tip-toed to the front of the room, creeping like a cartoon character so that he wouldn't hit anything, all the while stroking the wall with his palm to try and find a light switch. Weirdly enough, the only thing he felt was a pair of eyes watching him through the darkness. He whipped around to catch Rohan two beds down unsuccessfully hiding his snickers in the silence.

"Dude, you look so stupid right now," he wheezed gleefully in between fits of laughter. "You look like there's an egg in your ass and you're trying not to crack it."

"He looks like WHAT?" Laila hollered, twisting around in her own bed to lock onto Elijah's silhouette. Elijah wasn't even surprised anymore. Of course, he wasn't the only one that couldn't sleep. There was no point in sleuthing around if everyone was awake already anyway.

"I'm sorry, but that was just a very vivid description by Rohan," Laila explained. She looked Elijah up and down and snickered again. "And it looks like he was right."

"Y'all," Peter's impatient voice called from three beds away. "Shut up. Some of us are trying to sleep."

"Trying," enunciated Rohan. "I don't think anyone here actually slept a wink."

Now Cassidy stirred. "He's right. We might as well get up now."

"An egg in his ass," Laila cried. "Oh my god! I'm never going to forget that for as long as I live."

"Don't worry," Lars grunted. "You may not be around for very long with the way things are going."

A hush fell over the room. Whatever temporary joy or humor they found evaporated immediately, replaced instead with the implication of what Lars had just said. There was still a killer at large, and they were still trapped thousands of feet below sea level. That hadn't changed.

Elijah finally smacked something in the dark that resembled a light switch and flicked it on. There was an electric buzz in the air for a moment before the room was flooded with bright white light. Everyone groaned and put their hands above their eyes to shelter themselves from the harsh rays.

"Come on, y'all," Zach said while tilting his head off his pillow. "We should probably do a roll call."

"What for?" Laila questioned. "I heard everyone talking just now. The only person I didn't catch was Debra."

"I'm here!" Debra squeaked from behind.

Laila shrugged. "Then that's got to be everyone."

"Still," Zach pushed, "it only makes sense to check if anybody's wandered off."

A chorus of groans echoed throughout the room as the recruits jumped off of their respective beds and stretched. Elijah rubbed his eyes and went over to join Rohan and Laila near the center of the room, directly adjacent to where Sebastian irritably tried to stir his sister into getting out of bed. Finally, Debra caved and crawled out, joining everyone else in a line spreading side-to-side, eerily similar to the night before.

Only Zach remained, but he did not jump down to join the rest. Instead, he jumped on top of Elijah's bed and sat down cross-legged. He then began to count off everyone in the room before frowning. He counted again, mumbling everyone's names under his breath before frowning deeper than before.

"Someone's missing," he announced.

Everyone fell silent except for Sebastian, who cursed and rubbed his eyes with his palms.

"Count again, Zach," he advised.

"I did!" Zach insisted. "Look," he said, while pointing at Cassidy on the far side of the line. "I'll go in order. One." He pointed at Lars next. Then Sebastian. Then Debra. "Two. Three. Four."

This went on until he stopped at eight before turning his finger towards himself, finishing the count at an inconclusive "nine."

Elijah felt his heart rate quicken as he himself began to count everyone in the room. He found this task difficult as everyone else was doing the same thing, swiveling their necks around like bobbleheads to count everyone beside them.

Alas, Elijah and everyone else reached the same conclusion: someone was missing.

"Maybe they just went to the bathroom or something," Cassidy offered. It wasn't very reassuring.

"No," Zach said. "Nobody got up in the middle of the night. I would know. I was awake the entire time. The only time anybody got up was when Elijah crept across the room just now."

"Well, then who's missing?" Lars asked.

"Jacob!" Laila yelled suddenly. "Jacob's the missing person!"

She turned and started pacing out of the room before Elijah grabbed her by the back of her shirt, causing her to jolt and crash onto the floor.

"And where the hell do you think you're going?" Elijah asked.

Laila thrashed against his grip but gave up when she realized that it was of no use. She hissed through her teeth before sighing and sitting up.

"Jacob's got to be in the bathroom or something, so we could go over there and—"

"Laila," Rohan spoke this time. "Do you understand what you were about to do? I mean really, do you understand what you could've just cost us? How do you know he isn't the killer?"

Her silence answered his question. Elijah let go of her shirt and sat back against the wall. Laila rubbed her back and glared at him. He offered an apologetic shrug; she ignored it.

"Okay," Zach said. "Okay. Here's what we're going to do. We're sending four people out there to look for Jacob, and we're leaving five in here to look for clues as to where he went. Maybe there's something in his bag? I don't fully know, but four people have to go look for him." He scanned the room. "Who'll it be?"

"I'll go!" Elijah immediately offered. He was sick of being cooped up in that room, and the excitement of finally being able to walk around the submarine again outweighed his instinctive desire to stay with the pack.

Zach nodded his head and looked around. "Who else?"

To everyone's surprise, Peter raised his hand. Zach raised an eyebrow.

"Really, Peter?" Zach questioned. "You want to go look for Jacob?"

"Why?" Peter huffed. "You got an issue with that?"

"Um," interrupted Debra from her side of the room. Everyone turned to face her.

"I, uh, I actually do have an issue with that. Don't you guys remember what Peter did when he found the commanders?"

"She's right," Lars said. "I don't know if he needs any more search and rescue missions."

Peter's face turned a deep red hue as murmurs of agreement bubbled out of the nine recruits.

"For the last time," he said, struggling to keep his breathing steady, "I did that because it made more sense for both of them to be in one place. Why keep the corpses separate when we're all in danger?"

Zach shushed the room before anyone could counter Peter's argument.

"Look," Zach said. "We're sending four people on this little mission anyway. If Peter was the killer, he wouldn't get a shot without us knowing that it was him. Honestly, I'd say let him go."

Nobody disagreed, either out of agreement with Zach's words or lack of concern necessary to prolong the debate. Zach took the silence as consensus and was about to call for another person before Laila interrupted him.

"I'll go," she said. She turned to face Elijah. "As long as I get to stay with Elijah. I'm not going anywhere alone with Peter."

Out of nowhere, Elijah felt the urge to give Laila a fist bump out of the pure comradery of that statement. He resisted, however. There's a time and a place, and a mission to look for a missing crewmate wasn't it.

"And I'll go, too!" Cassidy announced. She excitedly dug through her bag and retrieved a flashlight. "In case the lights go off out of nowhere," she explained when everyone looked at her oddly. Her excitement was off-putting.

"Hey," he started, "weren't you completely opposed to setting foot outside the room just yesterday? Don't take this the wrong way, but you were acting like a complete, well, what's the word . . ."

"Coward," Rohan snorted.

"Right," Elijah continued. "Why the sudden change?"

Cassidy's face twisted with disgust.

"Okay, first of all, you're an asshole. Secondly, I *am* terrified out of my mind."

"Aren't we all?" Sebastian groaned. Debra elbowed him.

"But, if I'm being honest, it makes a lot more sense to stick with you guys than to be cooped up in a room of five not knowing what's going on outside these walls." She gestured around the room. "Besides, I do want to know where Jacob is."

"I think we can definitely rule out bathroom break by now," Rohan joked.

"That's four," Laila said. She stood and suddenly grabbed Elijah by the collar before hurling him towards the door. He nearly smashed into the wall before gaining his balance at the last minute. He turned to Laila with a bewildered expression. She smirked and shrugged her shoulders. "Payback."

Elijah winced and motioned for Peter and Cassidy to follow him. As Laila approached his side, he leaned over and whispered, "For the record, we are definitely not even."

She laughed a little. "Sure, Elijah. Sure."

They rounded the corner of the room and continued down the hall to a diverging hallway. One led to the left and the other to the right. Elijah frowned as they approached the division.

"Okay," he said. "We're either going together or we split into groups of two here."

Cassidy scoffed. "Yeah gang, let's split up!" she said sarcastically. "That's never been shown to go horribly wrong for everyone involved."

"She's right," Peter said. "We stick together."

There wasn't much else to say to that, so they turned the right corner and walked down the hall. The metal beneath their feet clanged and clanked as they trudged along. Elijah noticed the box he had smashed his shin against earlier and carefully circumvented it. He heard Cassidy snicker behind him.

"I guess you learned your lesson, huh?" she chided.

"I liked you better when you were a shivering frail mess," Elijah groaned.

"Hey, hey!" Laila butted in. "We're all friends here, remember? Let's just get Jacob and get out of here."

"Well, it's going to take forever if we keep going together," Peter said. His voice wasn't the gruff mess it usually was. He sounded like he was thinking long and hard before he spoke, which was something Elijah didn't think he'd ever see. "Maybe we should split into two groups."

Cassidy giggled aloud upon hearing that. "You're insane."

"Listen to me," Peter insisted. "Two groups of two. That means if anybody dies here, we'll know it was their partner. There's no logical sense in killing someone if everyone's going to know it was you afterward."

"What makes you think a killer would have any sense of logic after murdering our one hope back to the surface?" Elijah questioned. He turned to Laila, expecting a similar sneering response, but instead found her locked in thought. She kept that expression for a moment before turning to Elijah.

"I think he might actually have a point here," Laila said.

Cassidy's jaw dropped.

"No. No. We are *not* having this conversation. This is, like, every horror movie ever. Splitting up goes against common sense in every conceivable way." Her voice's pitch was increasing with every syllable by this point. "Have y'all never watched Friday the 13th?"

Peter shook his head.

"Ghostbusters?" she pleaded.

Laila and Elijah looked at each other awkwardly.

"Not even *Scooby-Doo?!*"

"Enough!" Peter bellowed. "We're wasting time. If we split up, we do it now. Who's going with whom?"

Laila pointed at Elijah and smirked. "I already called dibs."

Elijah pushed her arm away and turned to face Cassidy. "So, Cassidy, that means that you'll be going with . . ."

"You're joking," she interrupted. "This is a joke."

Elijah shrugged. "Sorry, man. You're with Peter."

Cassidy put her finger on her chin in a mock philosophical pose. "Hmm," she hummed. "No."

Laila rubbed her eyes and groaned. "What?"

"I said I'm good." She turned on her heel and started pacing back towards the quarters.

Elijah could feel his temper flaring up. Precious time was being wasted, and all of it led back to Cassidy's inability to get along with the group.

"Cassidy, please just get back here. You're making things so much harder than they need to be."

"Screw this," Peter said. "I'mma look for Jacob myself." He started towards the left corridor.

"Come on, Cassidy," Laila pleaded. "Weren't you the one talking about splitting up just two minutes ago?"

She didn't respond.

Laila sighed and grabbed Elijah's arm. "Screw it. We're still a team. Let's go."

That sudden change of plans flustered Elijah.

"What? I mean, shouldn't we at least wait for Zach to say something about Cassidy returning?"

"Zach isn't the boss, buddy," Laila groaned. "Now come on. As long as we don't split up, we'll be fine."

Elijah groaned. "Which way?"

"Right," Laila decided. "I'm not going near Peter."

"Fine with me."

She let go of his arm, and they began walking down the right hallway, winding up next to a few doors and hatches, one of which had a laminated sign on top that boldly declared in capital letters "STORAGE." Elijah grasped the doorknob and pushed, but the door was stuck. He pressed his weight against the door this time and threw himself against it, loosening it up a bit more.

"Hey, Elijah?" Laila asked. She was watching his actions with an inquisitive look.

"Hold on," Elijah panted. "Gimme a sec." With that, he began throwing himself against the door again, grunting with each impact. After almost a dozen attempts, he took a deep breath and sat down next to the door.

"It's hopeless," he said. "The thing's completely stuck."

"Oh, really?" Laila walked up to the door and placed her hand on the knob just as Elijah did, but she pulled instead. The door came open with a whine of protest, followed by several dust clouds that snuck their way up Elijah's nose. Before he knew it, his face was scrunched up, and he was sneezing violently like he had the flu. When the onslaught of sniffles finally faded, he looked up to see Laila with a face mixed with glee and disappointment. She offered a hand to Elijah, which Elijah grudgingly accepted.

"You know, you really do have an innate talent for finding yourself the center of attention in the worst ways. Like, there's being embarrassing, and then there's . . . you."

She waved her hands around when she said Elijah's name as though he were some magical deity whose ineptitude knew no bounds.

"Hilarious," Elijah said dryly.

He pushed Laila out of the way a little harder than necessary and walked into the storage room, cupping his hands over his nose and mouth to keep any dust clouds at bay. He searched the room, taking note of the various boxes and cabinets in the room, some with labels that were completely worn out.

"Hey, Laila!" Elijah called from inside the room. "Why don't you go look through the other doors. I got this area."

"Shouldn't we not be splitting up?" her voice called back.

"Stay in this hallway, and we'll be fine," Elijah responded.

He could hear her footsteps retreat into another door as he started eyeing up the room. It was obvious by now that Jacob wasn't here, but Elijah was still intrigued by the different boxes in the room. He pulled one box off the shelf and immediately felt his eyes water from the dust. Whatever was in this closet had evidently not been touched for weeks, if not longer. He held his breath and started looking through the cardboard box when he found a bottle of water.

Until this moment, he had no idea how thirsty he was. The stress of his situation and the missions he was on distracted him from it for a while. But now, the primal desire to chug the whole bottle was surfacing. There was a noise just outside the room, but Elijah paid no attention to it; all his focus was on the water. Quickly, he uncapped the bottle and lifted the neck to his mouth. Before he knew it, he was sipping air from an empty bottle. He dug around in the box again and took out another one and repeated the same action. Satisfied, he tossed both bottles backwards into the darkness and plopped the water box on the floor for later.

He went through the rest of the shelves and peered around but found nothing apart from some granola bars that had turned to paste, different colored toothbrushes with mold growing out of the brushy part, and magazine clips to guns that Elijah couldn't find anywhere in that room. After uncovering more and more revolting stuff, Elijah left and started walking over to the room Laila went in earlier. He was interrupted by another pair of footsteps coming the opposite direction.

"Laila?" he said. "Is that you?"

There was no answer, and the footsteps grew louder. Elijah clenched his fingers into a fist and walked backwards, feeling his heartbeat rise.

"Who's coming? Come on, answer me!"

"It's me, Zach!" a familiar voice called back.

Elijah straightened his back but didn't unclench his fists. He waited for the footsteps to approach faster until finally, Zach appeared around the corner, holding himself upright and beckoning for Elijah to follow him.

"What's going on?" Elijah asked. A drop of sweat fell from his hair onto the floor. "Why did you come here with no one?"

Zach held up his hand in a way that told Elijah that it was time to stop talking.

"I'll explain," Zach said, "but first, where's Laila?"

"She's off doing god-knows-what in one of those rooms," Elijah explained. "Can you please tell me what you're doing here now?"

Without saying anything, Zach started walking back the way he came, waving at Elijah to follow.

"Just follow me. Come on, Eli. We know each other from before. You can trust me."

The second those words left Zach's mouth, Elijah felt his hair stand up straight.

"No one calls me Eli, Zach," he huffed. "And we're acquaintances at best. With all the wisdom you were preaching about yesterday, I figured you'd be the first to understand that this isn't a situation where trust gets you very far."

Zach sighed.

"You cut me deep, Elijah." He said it sarcastically, but Elijah still couldn't be sure whether he truly meant it or not. "Well, I'm going to walk back now, and I heavily suggest you come with me. Bring Laila if you want, but something tells me this is something you're going to want to see."

"Could you please cut the riddles?" Elijah begged. He could feel his frustration rising and replacing his fight-or-flight reflex. "Just tell me what the hell it is!"

"Follow me," Zach repeated, "and you'll find out."

Now, here's the thing. Elijah had been trained as an AP recruit to follow any gut feeling he had and never stray from it. In this moment, his gut was telling him to put as much distance between Zach and himself as physically possible. The lines "We know each other" and "You can trust me" stirred a primal fear in him that he never felt before, except perhaps when his house went aflame. There was no reason, NO reason for Elijah to follow Zach. At the very least, there was no reason for him to not find Laila and get her to come with him to wherever Zach led him.

And yet, Elijah found himself putting one foot in front of the other and following Zach down the hall, cursing himself in his head for making such a textbook stupid decision. His legs were wobbling as he continued, almost as if his body was trying to sabotage his moronic decisions, but he pressed on regardless. As they began to round the corner leading back to the quarters, Elijah finally found the mental clarity to speak up.

"You have some explaining to do, Zach," Elijah said. "What were you doing looking for me?"

"I wanted to make sure you and Laila were okay," Zach explained. "Come to think of it, I didn't actually see Laila. You're confident that she's doing okay and just looking through those rooms?"

Elijah was taken aback.

"Are you accusing me of something, Zach?" He didn't get a reply back. "Fine. She's fine as far as I know."

"You better hope she is," Zach said unnervingly.

That sentence tipped Elijah over the edge. Before Zach could react, Elijah had grabbed the back of his shirt the same way he did to Laila and shoved him to the side. Zach's head slammed against the side of the metal wall and sent a screeching echo through the room, barely louder than Zach's following scream. Elijah took several deep breaths and started loosening up on Zach's shirt. He stepped back and allowed Zach to turn around, looking at Elijah with an expression of disgust and confusion.

"Listen to me," Elijah huffed, enunciating every word as he spoke. "Why did you come get me alone? Why are you acting so goddamn weird?" Elijah took a step closer to Zach's bruised face. "And why," he whispered, "are you so concerned for Laila's safety?"

Zach's gray eyes stared coldly back at Elijah before they both heard shuffling on the opposite side of the door to the quarters. With a quick glance at each other, Elijah stepped back and allowed Zach to pull hard on the door, yanking it open with a metallic groan. On the other side was Lars, eyeing the two with a raised eyebrow.

"You guys are aware that the door isn't thick enough to block sound, right?" Lars asked.

Zach ignored the question.

"Where's everyone else, Lars?"

"Sebastian and Debra are with her right now, and I'm pretty sure the Indian lad is taking Peter back here. Not sure how that works when Peter's twice his size, but that's what I got."

"His name is Rohan, Lars," Elijah chimed in. "Also, since Zach here won't tell me what the hell happened, could you at least fill me in?" Every word he spoke was drenched in spiteful sarcasm, but Elijah couldn't control his frustration—not anymore.

"Fine," Zach said. He turned to face Elijah and pointed to the red-purplish mark on his cheekbone, the result of Elijah smashing his face against the wall. "You'll have to explain how I got this to everyone, though."

"Sure," Elijah said impatiently. "Whatever."

"Okay." Zach inhaled and brought his hands to his mouth. He gave a knowing glance to Lars and, after what felt like hours, spoke. "Cassidy is unresponsive."

"Well, why didn't you tell me that earlier?" Elijah shouted before he processed what Zach had said. ". . . Also, what?"

"Yeah."

Elijah shook his head. "Yeah, what? Like, what happened to her?"

Zach opened his mouth to speak but was interrupted by Lars.

"Honestly, it might be better for you to see for yourself."

By this point, Elijah was too exhausted to protest. He simply let Lars lead him and Zach back through the hall and towards the left route. Elijah recognized the humming sounds of the engines and motors and realized he was walking towards the control room. However, just before they rounded the corner to approach it, Lars took a left into a closet similar to the one Elijah was rummaging through. Zach pushed ahead of Elijah and fumbled around in the dark until he flicked the light switch. With a delayed snap, the lamps flickered on and flooded Elijah's eyes with light. After adjusting to the brightness, he looked down to find Cassidy lying on the floor. There was a dent the size of a golf ball in the back of her head.

Without hesitation, Elijah flipped around and began pacing out the door, desperately trying to keep from throwing up. His head was swimming from the horrific sight he just encountered, but he could still make out Zach calling for him to stop walking. After a couple seconds, Elijah collapsed limply onto the wall. With unfathomable effort, he constricted his chest and forced the gags down, trying to think of anything but what he just saw.

Zach caught him by the shoulders, but Elijah reflexively pushed him off and slid back down on the wall. He thought of his house going up in flames, the day he met Rohan, and even the sleepless nights he used to have as a kid. All these memories, good or bad, helped block out the grotesque sight he saw long enough for Elijah to start asking questions.

"Why didn't you tell me straight up that Cassidy was like this?" he asked.

Zach gestured towards the room.

"There aren't a whole lot of ways to describe that verbally. What'd you want me to say?"

"Fine," Elijah said. "What about running over to me without warning? You didn't even bring someone else along like you've been saying nonstop to do."

"It was a bit of an emergency," Zach explained. "Come on, Elijah. Rohan had already left to look for Peter, and I . . ."

"Wait," Elijah interrupted in disbelief. "You sent Rohan to look for Peter alone?"

Now it was Zach's turn to be annoyed.

"I didn't send Rohan to do anything, Eli. He just left by himself. Lars tried to stop him, but he was already going back to the other rooms. And before you ask, Peter was away from Cassidy when we found her. It'd be pretty hard for him to hurt her that fast, but we're not ruling anything out."

Elijah racked his brain for questions, but nothing was coming to mind. Really, what was there to say?

"Whatever." Elijah was done talking to Zach. He wandered back into the room with Cassidy's body and shielding his eyes from the corpse. He caught sight of Lars through his peripheral vision. He seemed more melancholy than normal. It made sense, given the circumstances.

"Lars, how did this happen?"

"She got whacked. My guess is a crowbar. There's no sign of scuffle or nothing. It looks like somebody just smashed a crowbar into the back of her head once and left her like . . ." he waved his hands around Cassidy, ". . . that."

Now, the question that Elijah was afraid to ask. His throat clamped a bit before saying it.

"Is she alive?"

"Hasn't responded to anything we've done," Lars said. "There's a heartbeat, though. If you want to count that as alive, go ahead, but I don't think she's going to wake up anytime soon."

Elijah nodded. Surprisingly, he found that he didn't have any intense emotions about this development. Perhaps it was the fact that he was so tremendously emotionally exhausted, but his heart just couldn't give up the energy necessary to grieve. His mind felt like it had been throttled and thrown around like a punching bag, and he wanted nothing more than to sit down and soak it all in.

As he approached the quarters, he heard conversations on the other side. He rounded the corner to see Rohan and Peter talking with one another like they were buddies from college. Rohan was hanging upside down off his bed, and Peter was roaming the room. Elijah couldn't be sure, but he thought he heard Peter explaining his innocence to Rohan while the latter listened. Neither noticed Elijah enter the room until he spoke.

"Hey, guys," said Elijah. It was a stupid way to introduce himself after the events that had just unfolded, but frankly, he didn't care.

"Elijah!" Rohan yelled. Without skipping a beat, he jumped off the bed and ran up to Elijah like he was about to give him a bear hug.

"Rohan," Elijah said. "It's good to see you. I'm guessing you know about Cassidy?"

Rohan nodded slowly.

"And we still have no clue about Jacob. Man just vanished into thin air as far as we know."

He moved his shoulder to reveal Peter standing behind him facing the wall.

"I've just been here with Peter. Alone. Zach and Lars figured that if Peter was the one offing people, he wouldn't do it to me when everyone knew where I was."

"Y'know," Elijah sighed. "It's really sad how matter-of-factly you just said that sentence."

"Weird times," Rohan agreed. He stopped smiling and leaned in slightly towards Elijah's ear. "But between you and me," he whispered, motioning ever so slightly towards Peter, "I think he might be innocent."

Elijah thought about it. Peter volunteered to go look for Jacob, sure. He was down with the buddy system, which would have made getting away with murder needlessly difficult. He even got along somewhat well with the commanders before the bodies began piling up. But at the same time, Elijah couldn't allow himself to forget how emotionally unstable Peter was. His demeanor back on the surface couldn't be ruled out. Plus, according to Zach's story, Zach found Cassidy at a time when only Peter could've been in that hallway. Too many things weren't adding up.

Elijah was about to explain all that back to Rohan when his thoughts were interrupted by footsteps outside the hall. Within moments, Zach and Lars entered and veered towards Elijah and Rohan, leaving Peter and the Leagues in the corner.

"No sign of Jacob," Lars announced. "Zach and I couldn't find him in that hallway." His eyes narrowed as he began pointing around the room at everyone. "And from the looks of it, we have everyone here except Laila."

To everyone's surprise, Rohan giggled at that last statement.

"Sorry," he explained with a smile, "just getting deja vu from, like, two hours ago."

Elijah jutted his elbow into Rohan's abdomen before he realized what he was doing. With a heave, Rohan stumbled backward and fell on his bed, clutching his sides in pain.

"Shut up, Rohan," Elijah growled. "That wasn't funny."

Before Rohan could retort, footsteps began descending down the hall yet again, much to Elijah's relief. A second later, Laila was at the door, heaving breath after breath. Her hair was wild and unkempt, and her face was redder than the pills Elijah popped every night.

"Laila!" Zach said with a smile. "It's great to know you're safe."

Laila paid no attention to Zach and instead turned to Elijah and Rohan, eyes darting between the two. Elijah felt his heart drop before he even heard her speak. He knew Laila well, and whatever was going to come out of her mouth next would, to Elijah's intuition, be monumental.

As it turns out, he was right.

"It's Jacob."

CHAPTER EIGHT

ENGINEERS

It had been a while since Elijah knew tranquility. Well, maybe tranquility was too strong of a word to describe his feeling. Calm would be a better word. Since he entered the submarine, he had felt nothing but terror and anxiety for his life and his friends, but now, laying on his bed two hours after Laila shared the news about Jacob, he felt nothing at all. He was in more danger than ever, but truthfully, he didn't care. He didn't see any way to get out of his situation, so he just prayed everything would work out and kept counting the bumps in the metal ceiling above him. It was the best way to spend his time as far as he was concerned.

Jacob, to no one's surprise, was dead. Laila ran into him in the bathroom while Elijah was with Cassidy. He was sitting on the toilet fully clothed with a knife stuck in his chest so cleanly you would've thought it was placed there surgically. When Laila brought it back for everyone to inspect, Sebastian immediately noticed that—after cleaning away the blood and guts—it was exactly the same knife the recruits used every day at the base during mess hall. The next hour was a chaotic scramble of Rohan trying to comfort an emotionally exhausted Laila, Peter and Zach cleaning up Jacob and Cassidy's beds, and the Leagues and Lars outside of the quarters doing God knows what. Again, it didn't really matter to Elijah. He cared about his friends, sure, but there was nothing he could do to keep them from danger. There was nothing left to do but sit and wait for the inevitable.

For the next couple hours, Elijah continued to count the ceiling bumps absentmindedly. He got all the way to 1037 before he felt someone tap his shoulder. He turned over to see Rohan standing over him with his arm crossed across his chest.

"What's up?" Elijah asked.

Rohan squinted.

"That's what I was going to ask you. You've just been laying here doing nothing for three hours."

Elijah shrugged. "What is there to do?"

Rohan didn't respond to that.

"Follow me," he said. Then, mockingly, "Only if you feel like doing anything, that is."

Begrudgingly, Elijah got up and stretched before following Rohan out of the room. Rohan took a right turn to the same area Elijah went just a couple hours ago. Walking in that same hallway again, a shiver raced down Elijah's spine. He tapped on Rohan's shoulder and asked, "Where exactly are we going?"

"To get the rest of the water," Rohan answered. "Doesn't make a lot of sense to keep it here instead of at the quarters."

That made sense to Elijah. Before Laila and some of the others went to collect Jacob's body and put it with the others, Elijah had told them about the water he stumbled upon in the storage room. The second those words left his mouth, it was like everyone in the room suddenly realized that they were dying of thirst, and they all clawed to get out of the room to get some. Zach eventually calmed them down and forced Elijah to bring back some bottles for everyone to share. After that, things died down. Peter took out a bunch of MREs from his pack for everyone to eat. They tasted awful, but everyone was too busy scarfing down the subpar shredded beef to question it.

Regardless, that was in the past. Right now, Elijah had to help Rohan carry the boxes all the way back to the quarters. As they walked back into the dusty closet, Rohan gestured to a box of bottles on the shelf.

"We'll start with these."

Elijah nodded and bent over to grab the bottom of the box before he heard Rohan scoff. He looked up and raised his eyebrow.

"Something funny?"

"Yeah," Rohan admitted, "the way you're lifting up that box like a paralyzed baby chimp. Lift with your legs, moron."

"Shut up," Elijah bluntly responded.

The frown faded faster than usual, though. As he carried the boxes through the corridors, he thought about how nice it was to mess around with Rohan, even if he was the butt of the joke. It felt like so long ago when he could do that without feeling like something was weighing down his mind. He wondered if Rohan felt the same.

After a couple trips back and forth later, they had six boxes full of water bottles stacked around the entrance of the quarters. It was a nuisance to try and get around them, but Elijah and Rohan couldn't find any other empty space in the room.

"Hear me out," Rohan began. Elijah always hated when he started a sentence that way. "Maybe we could put it on someone's bed?"

Elijah knew what was coming but still wanted to give Rohan the benefit of the doubt.

"I'm not going to take up my bed space with these," Elijah innocently said. "And I don't think anyone else would take too kindly to that, either."

Rohan shifted uncomfortably. "No, no, I mean, y'know . . ." he sputtered out. Finally, he took a breath and laid it out. "There are . . . vacant beds now. It doesn't make sense to not use them."

At that point, another voice joined the conversation. From across the room, Debra gasped and straightened up in her bed.

"No. Absolutely not. We should keep the beds empty as a sign of respect."

Rohan sighed.

"Everyone's going to be tripping over these things, guys. It makes so much more sense to put them on a bed. Come on, Elijah," Rohan said while staring at him. "You agree, right?"

Elijah bit the inside of his cheek and shook his head.

"Sorry, man. It feels wrong."

Rohan turned now to Laila, who had been eavesdropping without saying a word.

"Laila," Rohan pleaded. "You don't want these boxes littering around everywhere, do you?"

Laila sighed and turned to face the group.

"For the record," she began, "it's not like I'm the tiebreaker here or anything. I don't care either way. But if you must know, I think there's going to be a lot more vacancies soon. We can figure it out then."

"Jeez," Debra winced. "That's dark, Laila."

Laila nodded and turned around again. There was silence in the room for a moment before Debra began tugging on her shoes and heading out the room. Elijah called out to her to stop, which she did.

"Where are you going?" he asked.

"To see my brother and the others," she said. She paused for a moment before saying, "You can come along too if you want."

Elijah didn't have anything better to do, so he picked himself up and followed Debra out of the room. Before he left, he turned back and looked at his two friends. Seeing them so unhappy made him feel like a coil was wrapped tightly around his heart and getting tighter by the minute.

"Hey, guys, you'll be fine alone, right?" he questioned.

Rohan looked up for a second and nodded while Laila didn't respond. Downcast, Elijah left the room and followed Debra down the left hall.

A minute later, he passed by the room where he saw Cassidy. He felt his neck tense up instinctively, even though he knew that the body had been moved. Some deep internal mechanism inside him refused to let him look for fear that her corpse would still be there. Still, when he heard rustling in the room, he looked in cautiously to see Peter dropping a bunch of cans and food packets off of the shelves and into a garbage bag. Rations for later.

Finally, Debra led him into the control room. The last time Elijah was here, the smell of the bodies stunk to high hell, but this time he found that his nostrils weren't twitching in agony. He noticed Sebastian and Lars hunched over the tiny computer screens and knobs throughout the room, so he stood off to the side.

"I, uh, don't know how to say this," Elijah said awkwardly, "but where are the bodies?"

Sebastian jumped up when Elijah spoke, evidently caught off-guard by his presence. While he was regaining his composure, his sister answered Elijah's question.

"Zach didn't tell you? He had Peter pick them up and place them in the closet area where CDR Brookes was supposed to sleep. They're all in there right now."

Elijah nodded. There wasn't much to add to that.

"What are you guys doing?" he asked Sebastian and Lars.

Lars looked up and wiped some sweat off his forehead.

"Remember how I was saying that I didn't even know if I could fix the radio, so why bother trying?"

Elijah frowned.

"Yeah? So?"

Lars shrugged.

"I figured it's better to find out if we have hope or not. Sebastian's helping me rewire and fix the damn thing, because whoever capped the commanders also made sure to slam this thing into oblivion."

"Not oblivion," Sebastian corrected while fiddling with a slew of different wires. "They probably didn't want to wake us, so they just pulled a bunch of random cords and left it at that. It's a mess to deal with, but not impossible."

Hearing this news, Elijah felt his apathy melt away. Until now, he didn't dare cling to the hope of making it out alive. He felt it was irrational and senseless. Now, hearing what Sebastian and Lars were saying, he felt a spark of hope ignite in his chest once again.

"So, what you're saying is that there's a chance we can communicate with the surface again?"

Lars nodded and smiled.

"We'll need more time, but it definitely looks that way."

Elijah stumbled back a bit before regaining his balance. Debra glanced at him with a concerned look but opted to help her brother rather than question Elijah's lightheadedness. She sat down, and the three began discussing the radio as if Elijah wasn't even in the room.

Filled with energy and feeling somewhat out of place, Elijah offered to help.

"Do you guys need anything right now?"

Sebastian laughed.

"Yeah, actually. We're pretty hungry. Can you get some of Peter's MREs?"

Lars glared at Sebastian, but Elijah didn't even notice that he was being ridiculed. He just turned on his heel and started running down the hall again to the quarters before rummaging through Peter's open bag. From behind, he heard Rohan warily ask, "What the hell are you doing?"

"Getting MREs for the guys at the control room," Elijah explained hastily. "They're trying to fix the radio as we speak."

Rohan froze.

"Did you say radio?"

Elijah grinned and nodded.

"Can't talk here right now, but you can come with me if you want to."

Rohan blinked twice, frozen.

"Are you kidding?!" he yelled. "YES! If there's any chance of me hearing . . . uh, hearing . . ." he struggled. He looked at the ground and scrunched up his face while thinking. "What's the name of the dude that's supposed to be monitoring us? Bane? Zander?"

"Zane," Laila corrected.

Both Rohan and Elijah turned to face her. She'd been quiet recently, likely a result of the same coping mechanism Elijah used, but he guessed hearing about the radio must've stirred something in her to speak.

"His name's Officer Zane. There's also Lieutenant Arnold, if I remember correctly. Where the hell they've been for the past day or two? I have no idea."

"To be honest," Rohan exclaimed giddily, "I couldn't care less who these people are. They're probably as confused as we are! The fact that we haven't sent them any transmissions must be worrying them, and if we can somehow get on the radio and—"

Elijah put his hands up and motioned for Rohan to slow down. His face was turning the shade of a tomato from speaking so fast, so he took a deep breath before speaking again.

"What I'm trying to say is, if we can get on that radio and let them know about the murders, they can help us out," he explained.

"I have no idea what the process is for saving a submarine actively miles underwater, but sure," Laila conceded. "Best idea I've heard so far." She slumped out of bed and picked herself up, fixed her hair, and looked back at the room they were in.

Elijah hadn't noticed until now, but Zach had been in the room the entire time. It had only occurred to him just now as he observed the room alongside his friends. Before he could say anything, he heard a snore rise and escape Zach's chest before descending back down. He turned back to Laila. He didn't even have to say anything for Laila to understand his request.

"I'm coming with y'all," she answered. "I don't feel too good about staying here by myself."

Elijah smiled. "Fine by me."

With that, he motioned for them to follow him and started running down the hall to the control room. He ran so quickly that when he finally made it, he almost knocked over the radio that everyone was working on. At the last second, however, he managed to contort himself so that he fell an inch away, saving the device (albeit at the cost of his dignity). Both League siblings looked at and shook their heads in disappointment while Lars continued to work as though Elijah wasn't even there. All he said was "Did you bring the MREs?"

Elijah nodded and placed them out around the group. Sebastian immediately picked one up and tore into it, finishing the whole thing in a rapid five minutes. During that time, Rohan and Laila had arrived and were looking around the radio, with Rohan, in particular, completely mesmerized as though he had never seen anything so spectacular in his life.

"So," Elijah said awkwardly. "How goes the progress?"

"Incredibly slow if you keep talking," Lars retorted. He then sighed and looked up. "You'll have to forgive us. This stuff isn't a joke."

"I completely get it," Elijah said. "Say the word, and we'll leave."

"We will?" Rohan asked, surprised. He corrected himself after receiving an intense glare from both Elijah and Laila. "I mean, uh, yeah. We will."

Debra, furiously tying up a group of wires, dissented.

"You can stay," she said, "but only if you help out. You see all those screens over there?"

The trio looked up and were met with twenty computer screens with old-timey computer jargon on them. They basically covered the entire front of the control room.

"Yeah," Laila said. "They're pretty hard to miss."

Debra didn't skip a beat.

"Go over there—no, over *there*—Christ, man, over by the blue screen," she tried to explain as Laila fumbled with which of the dozens of screens to look at. "Yeah. You got it. There's a knob on the desk in front of you directly adjacent to that screen. It looks like the type of thing you'd see on your grandma's radio. I need you to flip that no more than three times until you see the unit Hz pop up. You understand?" she said with increasing intensity. "Three times."

"Man," Rohan laughed. "I never knew you had an authoritative side, Debra."

This prompted Sebastian to look up with a borderline enraged expression.

"Now what the hell is that supposed to mean?" he demanded.

Debra tapped him on the shoulder and pointed at the radio.

"Forget about it, he didn't mean anything. Focus on the bigger picture." She waved her hand at Rohan, who was now shuffling around purposelessly. "Well," Debra said. "Are you just gonna stand there, or are you gonna get busy?"

Thus began a half hour of knob-twisting, input-changing, and wire-adjusting work. Lars and Debra spit out instructions lightning-fast while Sebastian worked, and the trio of friends tried to keep up in fear of being rebuked again. After finally plugging in the last cable, Elijah fell down, exhausted, and ready for a break.

Lars turned to glare at Elijah when he didn't immediately bounce back up.

"Excuse me," he said, "but I don't think we said you could sit down."

Elijah was about to complain that he couldn't feel his sides before Sebastian started screaming beside him. Purely out of instinct, Elijah jumped up and prepared to fight some murderous foe lurking in the shadows. After a second, however, he found himself staring at Sebastian, who apparently yelled not out of fear, but out of excitement.

"God, Sebastian," Laila whined, "you really can't be screaming like that at a time like this."

"I'm sorry, I'm sorry," he repeated. "It's just . . ." he faltered and pointed at the radio. "It buzzed."

Silence filled the room. Elijah and Laila looked at each other and shrugged, not knowing what Sebastian was getting so excited about. But when he saw Lars stare at Sebastian like he just found the Fountain of Youth, he knew something big was going down.

"It . . . buzzed?" stammered Lars. Sebastian nodded.

More silence. This time, Rohan stepped up with a question.

"What does that mean?" he asked. "Is that . . . bad?"

Sebastian shook his head. His eyes were almost bulging out of his head.

"No," he said simply. "No. It means there was a connection."

Elijah felt his heart jump up to his throat.

"A connection?"

Just as Sebastian was about to elaborate, there was a thud in the corridor. Everyone turned to look at the same time. They waited in anticipation for something to come forward, but nothing did.

"Some machine's acting up," Lars declared. "Sebastian, get back to—"

Then, out of nowhere, there was another thud farther away. Now everyone was as still as possible. For a brief moment, there was silence so loud it felt as though the room were about to explode. Elijah swore he heard an actual pin drop.

"Okay," Lars glanced around apprehensively. "So, what I was trying to—"

His sentence was interrupted by the unmistakable sound of a gunshot. The violent noise pierced everyone's ears and reverberated in their skulls. There was screaming in between the shots, a mix of anger and pleading coming from some indistinguishable voice. Someone in the quarters.

After pausing for just a moment, Elijah's brain shut off. He took off down the hallway, somewhat aware of Laila calling to him to stay back. He didn't feel his legs thud against the metal floor beneath him, nor did he feel his ears ring with furious intensity. He felt as though he were gliding through the air, free of presence of mind, free of thought. He felt the same way he felt when his house came burning down in New Mexico all those years ago.

In a second, he was at the corner of the hallway. He heard one final gunshot and a whimper of pain tumble from someone's mouth. He felt his heart race faster than ever before, he felt his arteries thump, and he felt his fingers tingle. Still in his delirious headspace, he wandered through the hall and into the quarters. In an instant, he took it all in. The gun. The blood. The panicked look on the assailant's face. Elijah could hardly believe it. After all this time.

He had finally caught the killer.

CHAPTER NINE

RED-HANDED

The assailant whimpered, "Now hang on. You . . . you don't get it. This isn't anything like what it looks like."

Elijah stared. He had a lingering suspicion from the beginning, but he never realized how obvious it was until he saw Peter's corpse laid out on the ground in front of him.

"He attacked me first," Zach pleaded.

His voice rose both in pitch and volume as he tried to make his case.

"He shot at me first! I didn't have a choice!"

He glanced down at his trembling hands, one of which held a pistol covered in both blood and tears. With a tense motion, he chucked the gun out of his hands and sent it flying toward Elijah. He looked up and tried to make eye contact, begging for understanding with his tear-soaked eyes. It made little impact.

At this point, Elijah felt his soul begin to recenter itself in his body. He became aware of the footsteps approaching rapidly behind him and the conglomerate of gasps and shrieks that erupted from his friends and allies alike. Counting Elijah, there were six people in that room, every one of whom was staring Zach down.

Lars made the first move. He moved closer, almost within swinging distance of Zach, and gestured toward Peter's body.

"Go sit on the bed in the corner," he ordered Zach. "Do it now."

After another pleading glance at the rest of the crew, Zach obeyed, shakingly walking to the end of the quarters. He sat down on the bed and buried his head in his lap, trying to escape the glares of everyone else.

Lars turned to look back at Elijah.

"Pick up the gun by the barrel and empty the magazine onto Peter's bed. Rohan, watch him."

Elijah did as he was told, robotically dumping the hot bullets out of the magazine and into his hands while Rohan watched on. After he was done, Lars looked back at Zach one last time before turning to face everyone else.

"What do you want to do with him?" he questioned.

Upon hearing that, Debra turned on her heel and walked out the door. Evidently, she wanted nothing to do with this. Whatever authority and confidence Debra had earlier at the control room had evaporated, just like that.

Sebastian gazed at his sister dismally before acknowledging Lars.

"Put him on trial? We have six people here, the radio is close to being finished, and if everything goes well, we'll probably be on the surface tomorrow night."

Laila shook her head.

"You guys aren't thinking clearly. He was holding the gun. Peter was the one screaming when we were in the control room. I mean, there's literal blood on his hands." She threw up her hands. "But hey, maybe he *is* innocent! It's not fair to rule it out immediately. But that's something we can worry about after we get back on the surface, not now when our priority should be the radio."

Elijah knew Laila was looking at him and trying to coerce him into agreeing with her, but he couldn't find the right thing to do no matter how hard he tried. Maybe it was the shock of just seeing his fifth dead body in the span of two days, but he couldn't think straight.

Luckily, Rohan spoke up next and gave Elijah some more time to focus.

"I'm with Sebastian, honestly," Rohan said, quickening his pace after receiving a dirty glare from Laila. "There's no telling how long it's going to take to get the radio fixed. It could be days, hell, weeks! We ought to hear his side of the story and judge him fairly in the meantime."

Elijah was a bit taken aback by Rohan's level-headedness, but he didn't have a chance to comment before Lars jumped right in.

"Zach killed a man today, whether he intended to or not. There's no empirical evidence pointing to his innocence, and the only eyewitness is dead. I say we lock him up in a room with food and water and wait until we get to the surface to decide what to do with him."

Elijah nodded before realizing that everyone in the room was now staring at him. He was the only one that hadn't voiced his opinion, and now he was the lone voice that could sway the vote. He felt Laila's gaze sear into the back of his head.

"Come on, Elijah," she said with a hand on his shoulder. "We've known each other since we could walk upright. You really don't trust me to make a judgment call?"

Rohan took offense to this and butted in.

"Ayo, Elijah," he started, half-glaring at Laila, "you've known me for a while, too. We're all good friends here. Don't let any of us sway you one way or the other. Pick the option that sounds just to you."

"I, uh," Elijah stammered.

The feeling of everyone staring at him, the knowledge that his choice could impact the future of the crew, and the trauma of having witnessed another death was all too much. His brain simply would not function.

"I can't decide," Elijah sorrowfully declared.

He tried to avoid Laila's disappointed stare.

"Then I will," Debra said.

Everyone whipped around to see her standing adjacent to her brother, wiping away the tears that had fallen down her cheeks.

"I vote with Laila and Lars. I even know a room that can be locked from the outside."

Sebastian frowned.

"Debra, what are you—"

She put her hand up, signaling for Sebastian to pipe down.

"I made up my mind. If Elijah can't vote, then that's the tiebreaker right there. Three-to-two."

Sebastian sighed and removed his sister's hand from his shoulder. Rohan and Lars eyed each other, and Elijah shifted around uncomfortably, but nobody argued against the verdict. Everyone turned around to face Zach, who had silently listened to the conversation the whole time. He looked up at them with the same helpless expression as before, but this time with a hint of anger.

"You really couldn't discuss my fate in another room?"

Debra shrugged.

"Why would we leave a murderer alone? We've seen how well that's worked out before."

Zach winced at being called a murderer.

"It was self-defense. You won't even hear my side of the story."

Laila sighed.

"Your innocence is for the people up above to figure out," she said. "If you're really not guilty, you won't connect to the other murders. Otherwise, I guess Peter is the killer. I don't know, and I don't really care right now." She turned to face Debra. "What jail room did you have in mind?"

Zach scoffed loudly, but no one paid him any attention.

"The closet right by the control room," Debra said. "We'll know where he is, there's plenty of food there, and we can check up on him whenever we want to."

"Y'know, I practically led all of you," Zach whined. Evidently, he wasn't going to let this go. "I was the de facto leader of this entire operation once the commanders dropped dead. Do you think I would've gone out of my way to make it impossible to kill everyone if I was the murderer?"

Laila picked up a tennis ball from her bag and chucked it directly at Zach's nose. He winced and fell back before glaring at his attacker.

"The gun was in your hands, Zach," she said coolly. "Now stop talking."

"What about the other attacks?" he continued. "I couldn't have possibly done all those. I have an alibi for Cassidy! Hell, I have one for Jacob! If I was going to pick off everyone one by one, why would I wrestle with Peter for a gun in the most public spot in this submarine?"

"Enough talk," Lars gruffly stated.

He walked over to Zach and picked him up by the crook of his arm. Zach protested some more, but it wasn't nearly as fervent as before.

"I'm going to pat you down to make sure you don't have anything else on you," Lars explained as he started to do just that. He frowned. "In hindsight, I probably should've done this earlier."

"It wouldn't make a difference since, y'know, I'm innocent," Zach retorted.

Lars just sighed and lifted Zach up before leading him out the room.

Before getting to the door, Lars looked back.

"Debra and Sebastian, you guys come with me. I don't suppose either of you have the key to that room?"

They both shook their heads. Rohan, however, reached into his pocket and pulled out a small silver key.

"Is it this one?" he asked.

Debra frowned. "Where on earth did you get that?"

"When everyone ran here, it fell out of your pocket. You should keep better track of your things."

Soon, the only people left in the quarters were Laila, Elijah, and Rohan. There was a palpable awkwardness in the air that was difficult to break through. While Elijah would usually find himself being completely at ease around his friends, he found that their latest decision to put Zach away was in the way of that comfort.

Rohan was the first to break the tension.

"So," he said, while fumbling with his fingers. "What do we do now?"

"I mean . . . I guess we got the killer?" Laila looked around, dazed. "Are we, like, safe?"

Every word she spoke had an edge of doubt stuck to the end, almost as if she didn't believe the words coming out of her own mouth.

Safe. That's a feeling Elijah could get used to.

"The way I see it," he explained, "it was Peter or Zach. Either Peter came onto Zach with the gun, and Zach fired in self-defense, or Zach straight up wacked Peter in plain view of us. Either way, Peter ain't breathing, and Zach's in a closet. We should be safe now."

Out of nowhere, Laila shouted so loudly Elijah physically took a step back in shock. Even Laila looked surprised at her own outburst before her expression changed to dismay.

"How the HELL did we forget about Peter?"

Elijah and Rohan glanced at each other in confusion, trying to figure out what Laila meant before their eyes rested on the figure on the floor.

"Oh, Christ," Rohan groaned, plopping himself down on Peter's bed. "How did we forget about the body?"

He looked up at Elijah and Laila in shame. Elijah had never seen this side of Rohan before, and the sight shook him to his core. Rohan's eyes began to water.

Was this really who they were now? Were they at a point where murder and the corpses of their friends were just . . . normal?

Elijah peered back at Peter's body. The tan uniform was stained crimson with the owner's blood, and the head was pressed into the floor, revealing only one side of his face. Elijah willed himself to feel something, to look into the eyes of his former adversary, and feel disgust, lament, horror.

Nothing. The only feeling Elijah felt was an empty tightness that threatened to crush his chest. He didn't feel the revulsion he felt at looking at Cassidy's body, nor CDR Brooks', nor CDR Patrick's. He just felt tired, as if he wanted to lie down, close his eyes, and never wake up again.

The trio sat like this, absorbing the situation in their own individual way, for what seemed like hours. No one dared look at each other, and the only sound in the room was the distant hum of an engine and the cracked sobs emitting from Rohan's throat. Finally, the sound of thudding footsteps entering the room broke the trance, and everyone turned to face Lars and the Leagues.

Sebastian looked around the room, frowning at everyone's expression of utter dismay.

"Is something wrong?"

Rohan's quiet sobs turned into laughter at that statement. His eyes were shut tight as he rocked back and forth in a fit of hysteric convulsions.

"Yes Sebastian. Everything is wrong with this."

Sebastian nodded, slightly put off by the maniacal laughter.

"Yeah," he agreed. He continued on as if nothing had happened. "Zach's in the closet next to the control room right now. There's food, water, and enough air for him to live for a day or two. Hopefully we'll be back on the surface before then so that he can stand trial alive."

Debra pushed her glasses up her nose.

"My brother, Lars, and I are going to get food for everyone, and then we're getting back to work on the radio. There's still much to do, but we're almost ready to send a signal out. It doesn't look like there's any other work that needs to be done."

Lars completed the group's announcements.

"Well," he said apprehensively, "there is the issue of the body. Usually, Peter would've taken care of that, but, well . . ." he tapered off. When nobody moved a muscle, Lars sighed. "Any volunteers want to take him to the corpse closet?"

Sebastian whipped around, furious.

"We do not call it that! What the hell is wrong with you?"

Lars shrugged. "It's an accurate name, no?"

Elijah couldn't fathom how this conversation could get any worse until Rohan spoke up.

"Elijah and I can take him," Rohan volunteered.

In disbelief, he turned and used every facial expression possible to communicate to Rohan that he did not sign up for this. However, his face did nothing but fold into one of grim acceptance when Lars sighed and said, "Good. Take him now, before he gets . . . messy."

"Messier," Debra corrected. Sebastian elbowed her in response.

Rohan motioned toward the body.

"Come on, Elijah," he grimaced. "We picked up all those boxes this morning; this is a cakewalk."

Elijah knew that Rohan was just trying to make the task at hand less miserable, but he still couldn't fathom how Rohan could say something like that with genuine sincerity. Regardless, he shut his eyes tight and slowly brushed his fingers against Peter's blood-soaked clothes. A jolt of nausea and fear shot up his spine, but he pressed on. Using his other hand, he picked up Peter by the back and started speed-walking down the hall with Rohan at the front, carrying the legs. His eyes were shut so tightly that tears began to leak.

"It's so cold," Rohan shuddered as they passed by the storage room Zach was locked in. Elijah realized a moment later that Rohan wasn't talking about the constant A/C running, but rather Peter's body temperature.

"Shut up, Rohan," Elijah spit. "Just stop talking until we get Peter in the pile."

The pile. Jesus. Elijah had to physically stop himself from throwing up in his mouth.

A second later, they were right there. Days before, Peter was the one that had taken care of the dirty work that was moving around the bodies. Now, in a twisted form of irony, Elijah and Rohan had to carry his body to the very same destination. It was a situation that should've driven them mad, but Elijah kept calm. He hoped that Rohan was keeping cool as well.

As soon as he finished that thought, Rohan took his arm away from Peter's leg and fumbled with the doorknob until it swung open.

Elijah was a smart man. He knew what was behind that door, and he knew well in advance to keep his eyes shut tight. Unfortunately, from the cries escaping Rohan's throat, it appeared that Rohan hadn't thought that far ahead. Elijah blocked it all out of his mind: the abominable stench, Rohan's gut-wrenching wails, and the feeling of Peter's frozen body. With considerable effort, Elijah felt around the corners of the doorway and shoved Peter's head in. A second later, he heard the legs tumble as Rohan followed suit.

"He's in there, he's in," Rohan gasped.

Elijah didn't hesitate upon hearing that; he dived forward and slammed the door shut. His breathing was uneven, and he could still feel Peter's frigid touch, but it was over. He turned to Rohan and put a hand on his shoulder.

"You forgot to look away, didn't you?" Elijah guessed.

Rohan fixed his posture and frowned, but it was obvious he was still processing what he had seen.

"The job's done," he said gruffly. "The body's disposed of. We can head back now."

Elijah sighed.

"Rohan," he insisted, "if you want to talk about things like this, that's okay. We're all going through the same thing here."

For a fraction of a second, Elijah watched Rohan's defenses go down. He could sense Rohan's shoulders relaxing, his eyes softening, and his head dropping. But just as soon as Rohan became vulnerable, he returned to his soldier-like position.

"Later," he dismissed. "Let's head back now." He paused. "Please."

Elijah didn't push it. Silently, the duo paced down the hall and turned the corner right beside Zach's room. As they passed, Elijah put his arm out and motioned for Rohan to stop. It felt a little too quiet inside the room. After taking a deep breath, Elijah knocked on the metal door.

"Zach?" he asked inquisitively. "You in there?"

His question was met with silence. Rohan tugged on his shoulder and tried to lead him away, but Elijah wouldn't budge.

"Zach, you doing alright?" he tried again.

"What do you care?" Zach's muffled voice responded. "You're just checking to make sure I didn't sneak through an air duct, aren't you?"

"Bro, you're in a storage closet in a submarine," Rohan said bluntly. "There aren't a whole lot of those in there."

A garbled scoff responded on the other side.

"Hey, Rohan," Zach said. "Anyone else there that wants to introduce themselves?"

"It's just us," Rohan assured Zach.

"Fine," Zach lamented. "You two weren't the ones that voted to put me here. I don't have anything against you two. But why would you go out of your way to come here? Are you trying to break me out or something?"

"No, no," Elijah hushed Zach. "Don't even say anything like that out loud. Nobody's here to do you any favors. We were just on our way back from . . . uh, from . . . y'know." His voice trailed off and fell into uncomfortable silence, broken only by Rohan's heavy sigh. Zach stirred on the other side of the door.

"Peter?" he asked in a monotone voice.

Elijah nodded wordlessly before realizing Zach couldn't see him.

"Yeah. Had to put him with the others."

More uncomfortable silence.

"Sounds awful," Zach said. Then, before Elijah could interrupt, he sped on, "I know there's nothing you can do for me now even if you wanted to, but I just need to know one thing. Please. Just tell me one thing."

Elijah was a little caught off guard by the sudden transition in the conversation.

"What?" he asked.

"Do you believe that I'm innocent?"

Just then, Rohan grabbed Elijah's sleeve and started down the hall.

"Alright, this has gone on for a little too long," he groaned while dragging Elijah away. His grip was strong enough to keep Elijah from fighting back, and frankly, Elijah was glad to have an excuse to get away from the situation.

"Elijah?" Zach exclaimed. His voice grew more panicked with every word. "Elijah! Do you trust me? Elijah!"

But Elijah didn't respond. He didn't see a reason to.

———————

The last time everybody was gathered in the quarters like this, it was to send a search party to look for Jacob. There was an air of anxiety for sure, but there was also a sense of optimism, hope that the killings would end with the commanders and that Jacob would be found. Perhaps there was even a childish feeling of excitement at the thought of snooping around a submarine looking for clues like an amateur sleuth.

Those feelings were long gone now. All that remained was a dull, empty, painful reminder that this may be the last time any of them wake up.

Elijah wearily flopped over and over in his bed, waiting for everyone to get settled before he reached for his sleeping pills. His brain was firing on all cylinders, absorbing any and all sensation that was going on in the room. He heard the shuffling in Laila's sheets, the cracking of Rohan's knuckles, and the snore erupting from Sebastian's chest. He turned over in his bed and felt his heart stop for a second after he saw Laila's eyes piercing at him through the darkness. They gazed at each other wordlessly, communicating in ways only lifelong friends could communicate. It almost felt like their eyes were talking to each other.

Are we safe now?

Is this the last time I see you or anybody else alive?

Will I wake up again?

A barrage of unanswerable questions tumbled out of Elijah's brain. Honestly, it felt cathartic to finally acknowledge the uncertainty that they were living in instead of pretending that everything was alright. Even if no words were spoken, he felt like he had just confessed his worst fears of the last few days to someone else. He guessed that Laila was probably experiencing the same relief, because soon after that non-verbal exchange, she closed her eyes and flipped back over in her bed. The rustling of her sheets stopped soon after.

Elijah waited for a few minutes before sighing with relief. At last, everyone was asleep or close enough to it that they wouldn't hear him rummage through his bag. He slipped his hand under the bed and reached around before snagging the zipper. The sound of the pull tab smacking against the bag was thunderous in the pin-drop silent room, so Elijah stopped to make sure he didn't wake anyone. When no one stirred, he continued.

Some painfully slow minutes later, Elijah had opened his bag wide enough to reach for the bottle. He rummaged through his bag, smacking his hand against dirty clothes and the like before finally coming to rest on the bottle. He stopped dead in his tracks. Something was wrong.

When Elijah pulled the bottle out of the bag, his suspicions were proven correct. A shiver raced down his spine as he scrutinized the bottle in the darkness. The bottle was empty. In disbelief, Elijah began shaking the bottle recklessly as if his eyes deceived him and the familiar clatter of pills bouncing around in the bottle would prove that they were still there. All he was met with, however, was more suffocated silence.

Elijah felt a familiar ache begin to ooze its way back into his brain. The last time Elijah put the pills back into his bag, he was certain that there were extra pills remaining. Now there were none. It didn't make any sense to him.

Shaking slightly, Elijah shoved the bag back underneath the bed and stared up at the ceiling. He wasn't even concerned about how the pills magically evaporated from the container more than he was worried about how he would end up falling asleep. He felt the frustration creeping back in, but he took a few deep breaths and tried to calm himself down. Maybe the chaos of the day caused him to forget where he kept the pills. Maybe he really did use all of them up earlier. Either way, they weren't there.

With a trembling hand, he reached in his jacket pocket and pulled out the only pill he had left. It was covered in dust and lint, but he didn't care. He plopped it in his mouth and forced it down his throat. He almost wound-up choking and waking everyone else up, but at last, he managed to maneuver it down. The pill count was now zero.

Elijah clenched his teeth and fists and groaned. The only thing left to do was wait for his friends to wake up. So, resigning himself to a wildly uncomfortable night, Elijah turned to face the wall and wrapped the blanket tightly around his chest, praying that sleep would grant him some temporary relief.

Chapter Ten

False Security

It took Elijah a few moments to realize that he had slept at all. The interior of the room was so devoid of light that when Elijah opened and closed his eyes, there was no difference. He blinked several times in a row in a trance before sitting upright in his bed. He had no recollection of the past few hours. Had he been asleep? Did he just zone out? Whatever the case, he knew that there was no going back for him. He rubbed his eyes and groaned softly before slipping out of bed and onto the metal floor.

It was difficult to orient oneself in such an environment, but Elijah made do. *Just don't crash into anybody,* he thought, *that's good enough.* With his hands up like a zombie, he felt his way around the room and finally caught the corner of a wall. He used his memory of the room to slink over to the light switch and flip it on.

Waves of blinding lights flooded the room and forced Elijah to cower momentarily. Once his eyes had adjusted somewhat, he peered through his hands and saw everyone shuffle out of their beds. A chorus of groans and whines echoed throughout the room as everyone else began to wake up. Blankets flew off of the beds as people clawed down onto the floor while cursing at Elijah.

Laila squinted through the light at Elijah before picking up the shoe beside her bed and chucking it at him.

"Christ, Elijah," she complained, "what time even is it?"

"Early," Rohan answered wearily. He got up and stretched his back so hard that an ensemble of spine cracks could be heard from across the room. "Way too early."

Elijah couldn't help but smile at their irritated grimaces.

"I don't know what time it is, but I figured the sooner we get that radio fixed, the better off we'll all be. If that means waking up at some ungodly hour, so be it."

Laila glared at Elijah with a look of absolute disbelief.

"Or did you just not sleep and figured that the rest of us should have to suffer with you?" she scoffed.

Elijah's smile wavered. She was the only one who knew about his sleeping meds, and they'd probably been friends long enough now that she'd suspected them to be the problem. Or, maybe, she was just messing with him. Either way, Elijah forced a smile back on his face.

"Maybe. Meet me in the control room."

Laila rolled her eyes. It was difficult to believe that just a few hours ago, they had no idea whether they would be going to sleep for the last time. Now, seeing Laila and all his friends safe and joking around filled Elijah with a sense of relief so powerful he almost felt like shedding a tear.

"Get a move on, then," Rohan jabbed as he pushed Elijah down the hall. Then, quieter, "You're becoming a mini-Zach with your orders, aren't ya?"

Zach. Hearing that name and, worse, being associated with it, made Elijah feel wildly uncomfortable.

"I'm not Zach," Elijah whispered in a more serious tone. "And speaking of which, we should probably check up on him once we get out of here."

"I agree," a new voice announced. Elijah turned to see Lars limping over to the group.

"Give the Leagues a second or two to get ready. Then, we can all head over there and finally fix the damn thing."

At this, Rohan frowned and gazed over Lars' shoulder.

"Where are they, anyway?"

Elijah turned yet again to see Debra furiously digging through her duffel bag in search of something. Everyone stared at her until she stopped and grabbed a pack of mint gum from the folds of a shirt in her bag. She looked up at everyone staring at her before frowning and shrugging her shoulders.

"Well, do you want some or not?" she questioned.

"I'll take one," Rohan immediately responded, "but first, go wake up your brother. Man's still fast asleep over there."

As it turned out, Rohan was right. While everyone else had already gotten up and prepared for the day ahead, Sebastian was still stuck in bed. Debra shook her head and walked over to his silhouette underneath the sheets.

"Oi," she yelled next to her brother. "Get up, Sebastian."

While Debra had grown more sure of herself as time had passed in the submarine, she still held a tone of patience and compassion for her brother. Unfortunately, he wasn't heeding her commands.

"Shake him or something," Laila said impatiently. "We don't have all day."

"Technically, we do," Elijah joked, but he wasn't smiling. Something was off about this whole situation. He felt a familiar anxiety creep in.

Finally, Debra had had enough. With one fell swoop, she swished the blanket off of her brother and put the back of her hand onto his exposed forehead.

"Dang, I can see why he doesn't want to get up," she jested. "He's freezing under here!"

Finally, she rolled Sebastian over so that his entire body was facing upward. For a moment, Debra stopped moving. She stepped back slowly, unintentionally obscuring everyone's vision of Sebastian. She took a deep breath.

Then, as if she had been thrown into a vat of boiling water, she shrieked with such force that Rohan physically lost balance and fell backward. Lars was suddenly by her side, guiding her away from her brother as Rohan looked around clueless and terrified. Laila had ventured to take a few cautious steps toward Sebastian, creeping as though she were sneaking up on a rabbit. And there Elijah was. Frozen.

No, no, no, he thought. He felt his head begin to throb with that familiar pain again. *No, no no. This can't be happening. Not again . . .*

While lost in his thoughts, his legs had decided to give into his morbid curiosity and move him closer to Sebastian's bed. Now shoulder to shoulder with Laila, the duo forced themselves to keep walking. Had it been just this morning that he thought they were safe?

Then, just like that, Sebastian was right in front of them. Just below his neatly-folded collar was a laceration traveling from one end of the neck to the other. Dried blood stained his body and clothes. His lifeless eyes stared deeply at nothing at all.

Without warning, a series of images began flashing through Elijah's head. CDR Brookes' and CDR Patrick's bodies lying on the control room floor. Cassidy's disfigured head. Peter's emotionless gaze. And now, Sebastian's empty eyes. All these images flooded Elijah's consciousness, and he at once became aware of how tired he was. *Of course, this isn't even close to over.*

Before he knew it, Laila was dragging him out of the quarters, leaving Rohan alone to process the events that had just transpired. Elijah followed Laila as she turned the corner to see Debra frantically sobbing while Lars attempted to calm her down.

"How could this have happened?" Lars muttered while holding Debra's head to his shoulder. "It's not possible, it's not . . ."

Just then, a wave of realization crashed over the group. They all looked at each other with wide eyes before Elijah said the name they were all collectively thinking.

"Zach."

In an instant, Elijah and Laila were flying down the hall to the jail closet Zach was trapped in. Immediately upon reaching the door, Laila tried the handle to no avail; it was locked. They had forgotten to get the key from the quarters. Elijah was about to turn back and get it before noticing Rohan sprinting down the hall opposite to him, key in hand.

"Here!" he exclaimed as he tossed the key into Elijah's shaking hands. When Elijah faltered, Rohan continued yelling, "Go on, go on, open the door!"

Elijah inserted the key into the door, twisted it furiously, and then slammed his shoulder against the door. It was difficult to detect, but the door was budging.

"Again, again!" Rohan insisted.

Elijah slammed into the door repeatedly, huffing for air each time. Inch by inch, the dust-covered door began to open, until finally with one last thud, it flew open to reveal a pitch-black room.

"Stay down, Zach!" Laila yelled as Elijah groped around the dark to find the light switch. They couldn't see him yet, but Elijah knew that if his suspicions were correct, Zach could do anything at this point. He felt incredibly vulnerable, but he pushed those thoughts out of his head until he finally found the switch. He flipped it on.

The lights took a second to obey, but after flickering on once or twice, the room became fully illuminated. Zach, too, became visible to the trio. Elijah's arm went limp as he processed what he was looking at.

Laila grunted in confusion.

"Oh." She approached Zach slowly, just as she did with Sebastian, and poked him with a foam cylinder laying against the doorframe. No reaction.

"That's, uh," Rohan stuttered. "That's certainly not what I was expecting."

Elijah knelt down and, after composing himself, laid his index and middle fingers against Zach's carotid artery. He willed his hand to stop shaking long enough to be able to check Zach's heart rate. He took a breath and stayed perfectly still.

"Well?" Laila cautiously prodded. "Is he . . . y'know . . ."

Elijah sighed and removed his hand from Zach's neck.

"It doesn't make sense. It really doesn't."

The trio sat in silence for a moment, pondering what could've caused all of this. Whatever explanation Elijah tried to come up with sounded ridiculous, and for good reason. There were two candidates for the killer: Peter or Zach. Both were acting suspicious and untrustworthy after Cassidy's death, but it was difficult to narrow down which one of them was the killer. That was, until Zach went ahead and murdered Peter in front of everyone, cementing him as the primary suspect. But as Elijah stared at Zach's body, he knew there was something he was missing. They were wrong.

Rohan was the one to break the silence.

"I feel like it's important to note that even if Zach wasn't dead right now, there is absolutely no way he could've gotten to Sebastian in time to silently kill him and then come back. The door was locked."

"Also," Laila piped in, "he's dead." When the other two stared at her unamused, she threw her hands up. "Hey, I'm just saying . . . that's a relevant thing to consider."

Elijah shook his head and stood up.

"Somebody killed Sebastian and Zach today," he announced. "That means one of us is still the killer. It means one of us has been framing Zach so that they could attack again while our guard was down. It means," Elijah sighed with defeat, "that we're still not safe."

"But it makes no sense," Rohan countered. "Why would they kill our primary suspect and not take out someone else in the quarters? I've seen how fast Debra falls asleep. He could've easily ended the Leagues tonight, but instead chose to do this."

"They," Elijah corrected.

Rohan frowned in confusion. "What?"

"You said 'he' could've killed off the Leagues," Elijah explained. "We don't know if the killer was male."

Rohan scoffed and walked out of the room, motioning for the other two to follow him.

"Elijah, there's two living girls down here. One of them is the victim's sister. The only other option for a female killer would be . . ."

He trailed off, and a feeling of awkwardness settled in as everyone processed the implications of what Rohan had said. Laila turned away, either out of disgust or disbelief, and started pacing down the hall towards the others. Elijah nodded in the direction she went and spoke, "Welp. Guess we should tell them what happened here."

"Yeah," Rohan said hurriedly, "let's do that."

They awkwardly shifted past each other and walked back over to the quarters. Before he even turned the corner, Elijah could hear Lars whispering with Laila, probably about Zach. They stopped talking when Elijah and Rohan entered and looked around the room. Debra was nowhere to be seen.

"She's over in the right hallway," Lars answered before Elijah could even ask the question. "It's probably best if no one goes over there right now."

Elijah nodded solemnly.

"So, you've heard about Zach?"

Lars shook his head and took a seat on the bed opposite of Sebastian.

"It doesn't make sense."

Having already had this conversation, the rest of the crew were silent. There was really nothing else to be said. Sebastian was murdered in the middle of the night, and the only person that could've been the culprit was dead as well. What else was there to think about?

Laila shifted away from the rest of the group and leaned her head into her hands, eyebrows creased in concentration. After a moment, she broke the silence.

"We all agree that this shouldn't be possible if Zach was the killer, right?"

Everyone in the room nodded slowly.

"So, the answer is pretty simple, then. It wasn't Zach." Her eyes traveled around the room as the weight of her words sank in. "One of us killed Sebastian."

Rohan groaned and flopped onto the bed behind him.

"No way," he scoffed. "Zach and Peter had their feud, and Zach came out alive, meaning only one of them could've been the killer. So, if Zach is dead—"

"Hold on," Lars interrupted with a sudden shout. "You never explained how Zach died." He eyed the trio suspiciously. "You're saying he just dropped dead in there? Just like that?" He didn't even try to hide his disbelief.

Now it was Elijah's turn to be impatient.

"He clearly suffocated or something like that. What were you guys thinking, locking him in an air-tight closet overnight?"

"I didn't hear much opposition from you, Elijah," Laila spit.

Elijah tried to ignore the animosity in her voice.

"It doesn't change the fact that there's a chance we, deliberately or not, killed Zach by locking him up in there."

"Then I guess we're all murderers," she responded spitefully.

"Guys, you GUYS!" Rohan yelled, standing up and stepping between the two of them. Elijah had no idea how quick his heart was beating and how tight his fist was curled until Rohan intervened. He took a shaky breath and stepped backward, purposefully averting his gaze from Laila's.

"Listen," Rohan began, "What happened with Zach is in the past—"

"Literally less than a day ago," Lars muttered under his breath.

Rohan continued without missing a beat, "—and we've got to look out for ourselves right now. Obviously, there's more than one murderer on this submarine; that's the only explanation for Peter's death. We should root out this other guy and figure out what to do with them from there."

Lars giggled, a response so out of place that Elijah physically did a double-take.

Lars apologized and explained himself, "I just found it funny. All we gotta do is 'catch them.' Simple. How exactly do we plan on doing that?"

No one could answer that. Instead, everyone turned to face Debra as she slinked back into the room, head downcast and arms crossed across her chest as if she were hugging herself. Her cheeks were stained with dried tears, and her glasses stood crooked on her face. She sat down silently on the floor, leaned back against the boxes of water and food, and tilted her head back. Everyone silently observed her, either with sympathy or apprehension, until Debra lifted her head and trained her unfeeling eyes on Lars.

Her voice sounded intensely gravelly as she began to speak. "We get the radio fixed," she hiccupped, "and we get to the surface. That's all we can do."

Elijah felt his heart sink when Debra spoke. Something about the way she was training herself to stay steady and unfeeling resonated with Elijah deeply, and he felt compelled to give her a hug and reassure her that it would all be okay. He didn't, though. That would be weird, not to mention untrue.

"I don't know if that will work, though," Lars rebutted, with a softer voice than before. "If this murderer strikes again and hits you or me, that radio isn't getting fixed."

"Woah, woah, woah," Rohan interrupted. He stood up and stepped closer to Laila and Elijah. "Why're you assuming that the killer has to be one of us?"

"Well, it's obviously not *her*," he said while motioning towards Debra. "And it ain't me. Process of elimination means that the killer has to be one of y'all."

"Enough," Laila growled. "It doesn't matter who the killer is. We have no method of determining who they are until someone else dies, so we might as well make as much progress on the radio as we can before that happens. In the meantime, everyone watch your back."

Lars smiled in disbelief.

"Hold on a second, bud," he said, "who made you the leader all of a sudden?"

Laila didn't even look at Lars as she stood to help Debra up.

"If you have a better plan, let us know. We'll be in the control room."

With that, Laila led Debra out of the room, but not before turning to face Elijah. She raised an eyebrow inquisitively, and he instantly understood what her eyes were asking.

"Rohan and I will stay back for a bit," Elijah responded. "We gotta get the food, water, and . . . 'Sebastian situation' sorted out."

Laila didn't even flinch at the weight of that statement, but she did nudge Debra a little closer to herself.

"Fine by me. Don't go anywhere else." She disappeared behind the corner of the room.

Elijah could see Rohan's reluctance, but he put a hand on his shoulder and turned him around to face the boxes.

"These have been crowding the entrance for way too long," Elijah started. "Let's get the easy stuff out of the way and move these."

Lars, who had been staring at the ceiling up until this point, sighed and looked at the duo.

"Oh, please do," he insisted. "I can't even count on my fingers anymore how many times these things have tripped me up."

"Man, that was my idea from the beginning," Rohan said in mock frustration. "I was the one that said we should just throw these on the beds. Why didn't we end up doing that, anyway?"

"I don't know, but we're doing it now," Elijah huffed as he picked up a box full of plastic water bottles. "Get the cans, Rohan," he gasped as he threw the box onto an empty bed.

Rohan, who was just about to lift the box full of canned goods, dropped it on the floor with a massive thud. Elijah whipped around to see Rohan staring back at him, fingers pointed at the box Elijah had just dismounted.

"What?" Elijah asked impatiently.

He could feel the frustration simmer in his breath. He wiped the sweat off of his forehead and went to pick up another box. Why Rohan was acting like this, he had no idea, but he wasn't going to let it hinder his progress.

Rohan's voice was solemn now. Any cheer from before had vanished.

"That bed," he explained. "That bed. That was Jacob's."

Elijah looked at the bed in confusion before a wave of realization crashed down on him. In reality, there was nothing but a box of water on the bed, but from Elijah's perspective, Jacob was lying down on the bed, staring off into space like he always did. There was real light in his eyes, and his face moved in such an authentic way that it was difficult to tell if Elijah was dreaming or not. Elijah blinked twice in awe and just as soon as the flashback came, it went. All that remained was a worn cardboard box.

Rohan sat down and rested his back against the box of cans.

"I think I remember why we didn't put the boxes up there earlier." He looked up at the dim lights on the ceiling. "It doesn't feel right plopping them onto beds where our friends were, like, three days ago."

"Jesus," Lars exclaimed. "It's really only been three days?"

Elijah, still somewhat shook from the flashback, stood and looked at both Rohan and Lars. Forcing his voice to keep steady, he offered the awkward ultimatum.

"Either we put these boxes on the bed or we don't. What do y'all choose?"

Rohan shrugged with an expressionless face before turning back to Elijah.

"What do you want to do?"

Without missing a beat, Elijah decided to be the authoritative figure for once.

"Put —'em on the beds. The dead can't trip over these things in the middle of the night. We can."

"Harsh." But he didn't dispute it.

Some huffing and grunting later, Elijah and Rohan had spread all the boxes around the beds of the deceased until there was only one left. Elijah side-eyed Sebastian's bed and sighed. It would take a ridiculous amount of willpower that Elijah simply didn't have to go anywhere near Sebastian's body. Rohan sensed Elijah's discomfort and didn't bother going for the last box. Rather, he turned to Lars and cleared his throat.

"Alright Lars," Rohan said. "It's time for you to pull some of your own weight."

Lars looked up inquisitively.

"What do you mean by that?"

"Elijah and I were the ones to take care of Peter earlier," Rohan explained. The memory of carrying out that task sent a shudder through Elijah's spine. "And since Debra and Laila are being productive with the radio, you have to be the one to put Sebastian away."

Elijah waited for Lars to burst into protest and refuse to do the job. Instead, Lars just sat in silence with a melancholy look on his face.

"Fine," he said stiffly. "But not in the corpse closet. I can't bear it."

This type of response was more than Rohan dared hope for, so he decided to negotiate.

"That works with me," Rohan said, "but we still need a place to put him."

Suddenly, Elijah got an idea.

"Why don't we put him with Zach?" he questioned. "That way we don't have to dispose of Zach either. We can just keep them together in the jail room."

"We're calling it the jail room now?" Lars cribbed.

Rohan rolled his eyes.

"Well, there's too many closets in this damn place to be specific every time. Just keep him in there and then meet us in the control room."

Lars shrugged and didn't respond again. Elijah threw a concerned look over to Rohan, but Rohan didn't reciprocate. He simply stepped over the last box of canned food, slipped past the jagged edge of one of the bed frames, and disappeared around the corner. Elijah, not wanting to spend another second alone with Lars, followed suit. Maybe it was just survival instinct, but Elijah didn't like the aura Lars was giving off.

As he followed Rohan through the left hallway and past the furnace room, Elijah seriously considered whether to bring up his suspicions about Lars with his friend. He knew how silly it was to be afraid to point fingers in a situation as dire as his, but he couldn't bring himself to say it regardless. Luckily for Elijah, Rohan brought the topic up first.

"You think it's Lars, don't you?" Rohan said matter-of-factly. He didn't even turn around when he said it. He just kept strolling as if they were casually walking to the mess hall back on the surface.

Elijah didn't know what to say. He trusted Zach as an ex-friend left on good terms, and that didn't work out so well. He knew Debra couldn't possibly be the killer, and he knew his friends far too well to even think about suspecting them. Then again, Lars was had a saint-like patience with the people around him. Elijah recalled the time he took a wrong turn absent-mindedly and stumbled across Lars and the Leagues working tirelessly on a laptop flashing green code across the screen. There was no mistaking the authentic look of leadership, compassion, and determination in Lars' eyes. He seemed genuinely invested in helping them learn, helping them grow.

And yet, here they were. It's like Lars had said just an hour prior, "process of elimination" meant that there was only one suspect, no matter how insane it sounded.

It was only when the duo entered the control room that Elijah realized he hadn't spoken. Forcing his body out of autopilot, he looked down at Rohan, who had been staring at Elijah for a moment before entering the room. Rohan nodded.

"Yeah. I do, too." Then, without waiting for Elijah to respond, he stepped over the ledge and announced their presence to Debra and Laila.

After seeing the condition of the radio, the wordless conversation he just had with Rohan was wiped from his mind. In just the past hour, there was now a recognizable radio where a mess of wire and antennae had previously lain. A step forward revealed the jumbled conglomerate of mechanisms spilling out behind the box, but otherwise it looked completely functional. Astonished, Elijah sat down and lowered his hand to touch the device when it was slapped away by Laila. Her expressions switched from serious to humored when she saw his reaction.

"You look surprised," she chuckled while flipping the radio over and meticulously prodding around the wiring. "I'd be insulted if you weren't so obviously impressed."

Elijah rolled his eyes and motioned for Rohan to take a closer look. While Rohan took his time fidgeting with the box, Elijah searched the room for Debra.

"Where is she?" he wondered aloud.

Laila looked confused.

"You can't hear her?" she asked earnestly. "She's behind the wall next to the closet."

She pointed confidently at the cement wall, confusing Elijah further. However, a second later, Debra came back around that wall carrying even more electronics in a ruined plastic tub. Elijah noticed the lack of emotion in her face and chose not to prod further. Sometimes, it's better to leave things unsaid.

Rohan, evidently, did not agree with that.

"You're ready to work again? Just like that?"

He didn't even try to hide his shock, but he quickly fell back into silence when Laila stared him down. Weirdly enough, Debra didn't seem to mind Rohan's comment. She just shrugged her shoulders and kept her head down as she disappeared back behind the wall again.

"She wants to be useful," Laila explained quietly after motioning for Rohan to come closer. "But you can't be saying crap like that. She's hanging on by a thread here, and I don't know how much longer that's going to last."

Elijah frowned.

"So, she's working to forget about her brother's death? That happened, like, three hours ago."

Laila stared at Elijah for a moment before leaning back and smiling.

"You remember the day after your house burned down?" she asked nonchalantly. Without waiting for a response, she continued. "The second the neighborhood kids and I got there, you and your family were huddled around each other and taking it all in. All of your memories, belongings, and sense of security whisked away by the ash and smoke. I don't think I even have to remind you what that day felt like. You thought you lost everything, didn't you? No one, not a soul, would blame you if you fell apart after something that tragic.

"You know what the funny thing is, though? The very next day, you and your parents were right back on your feet. You didn't mope.

You collected whatever you could salvage from the fire and took it outside. I remember looking out the window and seeing you and your parents carrying those boxes and tossing them onto the lawn. You weren't sobbing uncontrollably. You just did your job stone-faced until there was nothing left to do. Maybe that's because your parents never taught you how to grieve, but honestly, I don't think that's it. I think you just wanted to throw yourself at work so that you wouldn't have to think about the mess you were in. Like you wanted to avoid coming face to face with the catastrophe that just happened to you . . . I never brought it up earlier, but that's what it was, wasn't it?"

The only sound in the room at that point was the hum of the monitors and fluorescent lights above. Laila hadn't looked away yet, and something about her knowing gaze was so disarming that he couldn't bring himself to look away either. For that tiny moment in time, Elijah felt more vulnerable than he ever had.

Debra's approaching footsteps abruptly ended that moment, and everyone but Elijah turned to watch her come around the corner again. His mind was swimming with various thoughts and questions, but he forced himself to remain steady until he could talk to Laila alone. Being trapped in a submarine with diminishing supplies and sadistic murderers was a scenario that didn't leave much room for public emotional vulnerability.

"Okay," Rohan said slowly. "I don't mean to interrupt what's obviously a very sensitive moment . . . but did she just say your house burned down?"

Elijah sighed. He never got around to telling Rohan about the fire, and he could only imagine the utter confusion Rohan was in right now.

"We'll talk about it later," he said bluntly. "I mean it. Don't push."

In Debra's arms were another batch of supplies. After she dumped them on the floor next to Laila, she sat across from the radio and began looking at the backside where all the electrical components were spilling out from.

"The grid condenser is bent," she observed. "Twist it lightly upward and then put these in," she said as she held out two AA batteries.

Laila paid no attention to Debra's croaky voice.

"Damn," she muttered, "I feel like Lars would have a better handle on this than I do right now."

Right after saying so, the screw she had been trying to align clattered onto the floor, a consequence of her momentary loss of focus. She snapped her fingers at Rohan, "You, come over here and hold the radio still."

Rohan complied. Elijah felt dumb standing around and not helping, but he figured that if Laila needed help, she wouldn't hesitate to ask for it. He watched as beads of sweat collected on everyone's foreheads before a light twing noise echoed throughout the room. After freezing in disbelief, Laila laughed and sat back against the wall, huffing for air while fist pumping with a reluctant Debra. Elijah wasn't sure if he was crazy, but he swore that Debra's eyes began to look somewhat relaxed.

That could only mean good things, he thought.

As soon as that thought went through Elijah's brain, Lars burst into the room with something clattering around in his pockets. Everyone looked up at the same time to see him, but Debra was the first person to speak.

"Lars!" she exclaimed with a small smile. "Come over here, quick! Look at what Laila's managed to do."

"Yeah," Lars gasped, clearly uninterested in Debra's words. He wasn't paying attention to anything she was saying. "I just need to say something real quick."

"Say it later," Laila countered. "Check out what we've done first."

Lars was evidently taken aback by everyone's insistence to look at the radio, if not Debra's apparent excitement. After Elijah gave him a small nudge, he walked over and lightly pushed Rohan out of the way so he could get a better look. Within seconds, his eyes were widening with shock.

"How did you even manage this without Sebastian?" he asked incredulously. Elijah tried to ignore Debra's wince at her brother's name. "It took us a day to figure out there was a problem in the first place, and you manage to fix it in an hour?" He turned to stare at an amused Laila. "Who are you?"

Laila chuckled.

"Debra was the one pointing out what needed to be done. I was just the person moving the dials and rearranging the wires."

"She's being modest," Debra squeaked. "There was a lot more to it than that."

Lars shook his head and rested his palm on his forehead.

"Listen," he began quietly, "I don't know what you did, whether it was the wiring or the grid condenser, but the transmission LED isn't red anymore." He paused to let the update sink in. "It's green."

Elijah didn't know what that meant, but it sounded good. While he and Rohan looked dubiously at each other, Laila was pushing Lars out of the way to peer all around the radio.

"I don't see any LED," she muttered.

Debra, who had just received a massive burst of energy from Lars' statement, shoved Laila out of the way before carelessly rotating the radio downward.

"Oh my god," she gasped. Her hands began to shake in place. "Oh my god. It's green. The LED is green!"

To Elijah's surprise, Debra was grinning ear to ear at this revelation as if she was a little kid who'd just been gifted a puppy for Christmas. It made Elijah want to smile as well, but the memory of Sebastian's body quickly drowned out any joy.

"Hey guys," Rohan interrupted. "This is great and all, but can someone explain what the hell any of this even means?"

Lars was barely holding it together at this point. With slightly teary eyes, he managed to clear his throat and quack out, "We can receive transmissions from the surface."

Pin-drop silence. It was as if the world itself came to an abrupt halt so that everyone could process what Lars was saying individually. Elijah, who had been standing beside the door for the past few minutes, creeped forward and rested his hand on the antennae of the radio before turning to Lars. He was terrified to ask the question on his mind, but he mustered up the courage anyway.

"You're telling me," he whispered, "that this thing can communicate with the station on the surface?"

Lars didn't have to say anything. All he did was smile warmly and nod.

The room exploded into pandemonium. Laila and Debra hugged gleefully, Rohan stood and hollered for joy, and Elijah fell back in utter bafflement. That radio, that damn radio, the size of a shoe box and the color of coal had tormented them all for so long, inviting hope and the possibility of rescue to them all while simultaneously keeping it out of reach with its inoperative structure. Friends and allies alike had fallen while this radio stood firm, refusing to cooperate, refusing to help. Now, after all the terror and pain, Lars was saying there was a chance. Rescue wasn't a shot-in-the-dark hope anymore. The possibility was real now. Tangible.

Elijah looked up, expecting Lars' face to mirror the relief and excitement so palpable in the room. Oddly enough, Lars looked tense.

Maybe he's still worried about the killer, Elijah thought, but he still asked the question. "What's up with you, Lars? Aren't you happy?"

"No, it's not that." He shuffled over to the doorway and sighed. "I found something when I was in the jail closet."

Debra finally let go of Laila's embrace and spoke. "What were you doing in there?"

Either out of impatience or empathy, Lars ignored her.

"When I was in there, moving around . . . uh, a piece of cargo, I felt something on the side of Zach's jacket pocket."

"Wait," Debra interrupted. "What were you possibly doing that could've led you to touching Zach's pockets?"

"Debra," Laila said reassuringly. "Not now."

Elijah respected her calm demeanor. Somehow, Laila knew what "cargo" they were referring to, and she wanted to save Debra from picturing that image.

"Anyway, I just brushed up against something and decided to see what it was. I know I probably should've called one of you, but I didn't think much back then."

"Hey, this is great and all," Rohan chimed in, "but we have a fully functional radio right here. Is this really so important that it takes priority over that?"

"Let me finish." He turned to Elijah, sending a shiver down his back for some odd reason. "You were the one to check if Zach was dead, right?"

Elijah nodded, wondering where he was going with this.

"Were you able to figure out how he died? Or did y'all just assume he asphyxiated or something in there?"

Elijah shook his head, confused as to why Lars would be asking these questions. Luckily, Lars had finally gotten to the point.

"I don't think he suffocated, you guys," he said. As he was talking, he reached into his pocket and pulled something out. Something that made an all-too-familiar rattling noise. Something that made Elijah's heart both rise with recognition and sink with bewilderment.

Lars opened his hands to reveal four tiny red pills in his palm. Pills that Elijah had used every day for as long as he'd had insomnia. Pills that Elijah could not fathom being in the pocket of one of his dead crewmates.

"Zach didn't suffocate," Lars repeated. He paused for a moment, making sure everyone in the room understood the full weight of his words. "He overdosed."

CHAPTER ELEVEN

SEEDS OF DISTRUST

In the span of five seconds, the radio was shoved to the back of everyone's minds. The only thing that mattered now were the pills shining in Lars' hand, an image so surreal Elijah was almost convinced that he was dreaming. His pills . . . what were they doing with Lars? His face dropped as he connected the dots. The more important question was . . . what were they doing with Zach?

"Lars." Laila's voice was just above a whisper. "We were there. There was nothing wrong with him. He didn't have a single wound, injury, not even a tiny blemish. If he overdosed, we would've known."

"There's always a chance you missed something," Lars insisted. "Think about it. Zach had these in his pockets when he died, and I'm pretty sure if he was going to run out of air, he would've screamed for help earlier, or at the very least, he would have made *some* noise. Come on, Elijah. How much do you want to bet that you just missed something when you were looking Zach over?"

Elijah couldn't hear anything Lars was saying. He was too focused on not breaking down in front of everyone. Despite his best attempts, his breathing was rapid, his face was tomato-red, and his hands were visibly shaking. Everyone was looking at him, and he knew it, but he couldn't bring himself to stop.

"Yo. Elijah?"

That's why there weren't any pills left last night. That's why Zach mysteriously dropped dead. Then, maybe he could have taken them after murdering Sebastian? Wait, no, how would he have gotten out of the closet? Hell, how'd he get his goddamn hands on MY goddamn pills in the first place?

"ELIJAH!" Lars' thunderous voice snapped Elijah out of his trance-like state. He looked up and tried breathlessly to speak, to explain himself. However, a second later, he realized that no one knew that those pills were his. He kept them hidden from everyone every single night without fail, right? Then . . . no one suspected him after all! Still, he had to play off his nervous breakdown just now. No matter. *Now is the time to stay collected. Just talk.*

"I checked him," Elijah muttered unconfidently. He cleared his throat and spoke again, his voice sharper this time. "And I didn't find a single pill on him. Granted, I didn't go out of my way to check his pockets, but I'm not so sure about him overdosing. Where would he even get drugs from in a submarine?"

Lars put his head down and pondered what Elijah said.

They were buying it. Good.

"Hey, bud," Rohan interjected. "I don't mean to interrupt, but are you doing alright? You looked like you saw a ghost just now."

"What? Nah, man, I'm fine. It's just really concerning how a bunch of drugs ended up in Zach's pockets. It opens up a whole 'nother can of worms we can't handle right now."

Oh my god. He had never felt such a rush of adrenaline before. His speech was so fluent and casual that he almost felt ashamed of his incredible ability to cover for himself. Still, any guilt he felt about lying directly to his friend was stomped out by the reminder that he had to keep up the act until they moved on to something else.

All that time, Lars was still deep in thought. His hands rested on the sides of the table beside him, and a single pill fell through a gap in his fist and onto the floor. Everyone watched as it rolled leisurely across the room before, to Elijah's relief, lightly tapping the radio.

For a solid minute, everyone quietly gazed at the pill. Debra, who had stayed next to the radio the entire time Lars was speaking, picked it up and meticulously placed it on the edge of a nearby keyboard. She looked at the others for a moment before speaking softly, "Lars, can you do something for me?"

Lars looked a little taken aback, but he nodded.

Debra cleared her throat. "Can you go and check that these pills aren't on Sebastian?"

Elijah felt like he'd been slapped in the face. With all the chaos of the radio and his pills, he had forgotten that Debra had just lost her brother. He watched as Lars grunted affirmatively before slinking out of the room. When no one was looking, he snatched the pill off the keyboard and stuffed it in his breast pocket. There were bits of hair and dust on it, but he didn't care. If he had to stay down here for another night, he would need it.

"What are you going to do with that?" Rohan questioned.

"It's evidence. I'll hold onto it until we get to the surface so that forensics can have a look. No point in letting it collect dust next to a keyboard."

Rohan nodded, but Elijah could still see an inkling of distrust in his eyes. He decided to change the subject.

"Debra," Elijah said while pointing at the radio, "let's get this thing up and running. If we can contact the surface, we have to do it now."

Debra nodded and immediately got to work. Her depression began to melt away visibly with every tweak she made to the radio: pushing buttons no one could see, aligning the power adapter, or rearranging wires until finally she confidently began to turn the dial on the front of the radio, unleashing a garbled audio monstrosity into the room. While everyone else slammed their hands on their ears, Debra carefully picked up the box and slid the wires through a hole in the metal wall before finally slipping the radio through the box-shaped hole in the shelf adjacent to Laila. A moment later, the screeches of the transmission halted and gave way to softer—albeit irregular—noise.

"Oh my god," Lars gasped, revealing his presence in the doorway. He shook his head at Debra, who turned away and kept fidgeting with the radio. There were no pills on Sebastian after all. Lars continued, "I haven't heard a noise that blissful in years."

"Really?" Rohan stared in disbelief. "I'll be honest, that noise sounds like the feeling I get when I stub my toe in the middle of the night."

Lars smiled. "It's about what it represents. That garbage noise means that, however weak it may be, we can receive and send transmissions to the surface. Once Debra and I figure out the right frequency—"

"Done," Debra announced.

Lars whipped around so fast, the glasses on the bridge of his nose flew off and nearly smashed into the wall. Everyone in the room took a step back.

"What?"

"I said I'm done. I remember the dial from the navigation bootcamp, remember? The one with you, me, and CDR Patrick?"

Lars snapped his fingers and began grinning ear-to-ear.

"The one where you replaced your brother! I do remember!" He stepped over to the radio as he spoke. "So, this means . . . we're on the frequency now?"

Debra nodded. Elijah tried to make eye contact with his friends to see their reactions, but everyone was laser-focused on the radio. There was an understanding that whatever Debra was talking about, it was their key to escaping the hell they'd been trapped in for the past three days. A hush fell over the room as Debra hovered her finger over the tiny white button below the dial. She took the longest, fullest breath Elijah had ever seen before pushing the button and stepping back.

For a moment, nothing happened. The only thing that changed was the feeling of suspense lingering in the room. The radio continued to crackle and spew garbage audio like before, and Elijah could feel his heart beat faster. This had to work. This was their one chance to stop the suffering. This was their one opportunity to get out.

The radio continued to sputter. Then, it began to sputter slightly softer. The volume of the noise continued to diminish until it was barely audible, like listening to a TV through a wall. Everyone stared at Debra to see if that was supposed to happen. Unfortunately, her face remained focused and still, giving no hints one way or the other.

And then, there was a voice. It was difficult to distinguish at first because of how muffled and garbled it sounded, but real human words were forming on the other side of the radio.

"Kkrewwkkgh. Hhhlo? Kkkreegh."

Everyone froze.

"Krewwgh! Rger if lin connect? Iden-krree-fy sbmarin?"

"IT WORKS!!" Lars screeched with joy.

In the blink of an eye, he was already across the room and hugging Debra in glee. The juxtaposition between his thrilled face and Debra's stunned expression was hilarious, but Elijah hardly focused on that now.

"You guys!" Laila bellowed at Lars and Debra. "Fix the damn thing so we can understand what he's saying!"

Debra and Lars locked eyes and nodded. Together, they jumped over to the radio and began fixing and twisting various components. Debra would flip a lever in the back, and the radio would return to its original state of garbage noise. Lars would push her and move a dial, and the volume of the radio would explode throughout the room. They continued to fidget desperately with it for a minute while Elijah, Rohan, and Laila looked back and forth at each other with indescribable emotion. Honestly, Elijah struggled to verbalize how he felt, too. He almost thought he was dreaming

Finally, Debra and Lars pulled away and paused, the both of them huffing and puffing as though they had just completed a marathon. Their backs were turned to the rest of the group, but Elijah could tell by their body language that something was off. He was about to question why they stopped before Debra slapped her forehead and, once again, shoved Lars out of the way.

"Idiot!" she murmured as she fiddled with the antennae. "How did we forget?"

Upon pointing it upward, she creeped back cautiously like she was being stalked by a mountain lion. She stopped once she reached the other side of the room, and for a moment, the only noise in the room was the continued screech of the radio. And then, the silence was broken. A voice erupted from the wall, clear and crisp in sound.

"Hello?"

No one said a word.

"Hello? Does anyone copy?" The voice sighed and began increasing in volume. "Damn it, does anyone hear me?"

The answer came in the form of a chorus of screaming, crying, and hysterical laughter. It was difficult to make out who was doing what through all the tears coating Elijah's eyes, but he could make out Laila screaming with joy, Rohan staring blankly into space, and Lars and Debra hugging each other as they jumped up and down. As for Elijah? He sat still and looked around silently as he took it all in. He had seen things no one could ever unsee, and he had become desensitized to things far too inhumane for anyone, let alone a recruit. Hearing the Lieutenant on the other side of the radio filled Elijah with neither hope nor jubilation. Instead, it emptied him of the pain he had been holding onto for the past few days.

And Elijah was grateful. There was still no guarantee that he and his friends would make it out of here alive, but hearing a familiar voice from up above was enough for now. Yes. For now, everything was right.

The following hour or so was a haze of conversation between Lars and Lieutenant Arnold. A constant stream of questions came from both sides.

What happened to the commanders? Is anyone worried about us? What depth are you at? When can you get us out?

Neither could seem to answer the other before another question popped in mind.

At this point, everyone sat and rested apart from Lars and Debra, the latter of whom was rushing around the room to find geographic data to send to Arnold. Bored, Elijah's mind wandered to an old book his mother used to read to him when he was very young, at most eight years old. It was a classic tale of a knight slaying a dragon and conquering evil, the kind of book you'd find in the bargain bin at a Scholastic Book Fair. Anyway, after all was said and done, the book abruptly ended with the knight riding home in a brilliant blanket of sunlight, cloaked in pride and heroism after accomplishing his sacred mission.

Elijah remembered how every time his mom finished the story, he would always ask the same question: "What happened after? What did the knight do once he made it out alive and got back home?"

Elijah smiled slightly. Now, he knew. Or at the very least, he would find out very, very soon.

Minutes later, Laila started stretching her arms and motioning to get up. Elijah gazed over at her and tried to catch her eye, but she wouldn't look in his direction. He tried again, staring intently at her as she started moving towards the door, but her eyes seemed curiously locked on the floor. He frowned as he sat up to follow her.

He and Laila had been friends for so long that they could communicate through their eyes, often more effectively than through their words. That's how they had an entire dialogue in seconds when they heard Zach fire the shot that killed Peter. It was how they expressed their deep dread and paranoia when they went to sleep that same night. When you have a friendship as solid as theirs, you don't even need to talk to each other to understand certain things. So, for her to exit the room without a word with her eyes glued to the floor? Elijah frowned. Something else was going on.

As he left the control room, he noticed that Laila was standing still, arms crossed and back turned to him. This only confirmed Elijah's suspicions, so he decided to pry.

"Hey, what's up?"

Laila didn't respond verbally but instead gave the courtesy of turning to face him. Her eyes remained glued to the floor. Elijah was beginning to grow concerned, so he dropped the mask of ignorance.

"Laila, what's wrong?"

Finally, she looked him in the eyes.

"What were your pills doing in Zach's pockets, Elijah?"

Of all the things he was expecting to hear, THAT was not one of them. He felt his entire soul recoil, his posture slump, and his head hang loose as he began to realize the obvious: Laila knew.

Of course, she did! His insomnia was one of the first things she ever learned about him, before she even knew when his birthday was or where he lived. Elijah had to physically restrain himself from slapping his forehead. How could he have been so stupid to believe that he could get away with pretending the pills weren't his? How could he have forgotten about Laila?

The next words that came out of his mouth surprised the both of them.

"Why didn't you say anything earlier?"

Laila raised an eyebrow.

"I dunno. I thought you had an explanation, I guess. But then you went and acted like they weren't yours." She squinted at him suspiciously. "Tell me. What was that about?"

Crap. She was right.

"I don't know how the hell they got into Zach's pocket, honest. I don't know if Lars planted them or if Zach really did OD on them . . . I just don't know. But I didn't give any to him or anyone else. There were pills missing from the bottle when I woke up this morning, but I didn't mention that."

"Why not?"

"What do you mean 'why not,' Laila? God." He turned around in frustration. "How could I possibly bring it up without revealing that I got issues sleeping? The last thing I need is for these people to think I'm some kind of deranged insomniac when people are dying. They'd think I'm crazy!"

Laila didn't respond. All she did was frown and stare at the bridge of Elijah's nose, either in frustration or deep thought. The sight made Elijah delirious.

"Laila. Laila, please say something."

She sighed.

"You were the one that looked over Zach's corpse. You checked his pulse. He had your pills in his pocket. And on top of ALL of that, you lied about it to everyone several times without batting an eye."

"Oh, come ON. You and I both know how unfair you're being."

Laila's frown began to transition into a look of unease, perhaps even guilt.

"Maybe," she responded. "I'm sorry. I know you can't possibly be the killer."

Elijah rolled his eyes.

"It's really disappointing that you had to think about that at all, honestly."

Laila pursed her lips.

"Elijah, you have to stop joking around. We can't afford it anymore. I trust you and Rohan, and I really don't think it could've been Debra. Lars has been nothing but helpful this entire time, and he has an alibi for essentially every murder."

"What're you getting at?"

Laila shrugged defensively. "I don't know. I don't know anything anymore! That's the point!"

Out of the blue, Elijah reached his hand out and lifted Laila's chin so that she was looking him in the eyes again. What would've otherwise been an overtly romantic gesture felt completely natural in that moment.

"Hey," Elijah said softly. "We'll be okay."

Laila forced a smile while pushing his hand off her face at the same time.

"Sure." She paused, took a deep breath, and allowed her face to return to a melancholy expression. "Hey, Elijah?"

"Yeah?"

"I can trust you, right?"

Oddly enough, he didn't feel offended by the question. She had good reason to doubt him, and Elijah wouldn't blame her if she did. It would hurt, no doubt, but he still wouldn't blame her.

"I don't know. Do you think you can trust me?"

Laila didn't falter.

"Yes. At least, I hope so."

Elijah smiled.

"Good. Now come on. It's a wonder that nobody's looking for us right now."

He reached out his hand for her to grab and led her back into the control room. With each step he took, he felt a little lighter. He finally figured out what the weight on his shoulders was, and he had done away with it. Now, all he had to do was wait to be rescued. Then everything would finally be back to normal.

"Ay," Rohan shouted as they reentered the room. "Are you guys okay?"

"Yeah, we're fine," Elijah insisted.

Rohan shrugged and went back to staring at nothing. Elijah smiled a little and went back to his previous spot. Just as he was about to sit down, the radio crackled back to life. He didn't quite catch what Arnold had said, but from the look of relief on Debra's face, he assumed that it had to be good.

"They're sending a DSRV for us either tomorrow or the day after," she said tiredly. "In the meantime, he told us to just stay together and never venture off alone."

Rohan smirked.

"Tell that to Laila and Elijah," he said. "They went outside just now and never explained why."

"We were thirsty," Elijah said bluntly without looking anyone in the eye. Changing the subject, he asked Debra, "What the hell is a DSRV?"

Debra shrugged and flopped down into a chair.

"I don't know, man. I think he said it was some kind of rescue vehicle. Did you say you were thirsty?"

"I'm STARVING," Lars interjected before flipping a switch on the radio that severed the incoming audio stream. "Let's get some food."

Rohan hollered mockingly. "Hooray! Another day of crusty, dry, putrid MREs. Can't wait to put another one of those in my body."

"Chill out," Elijah countered as he stood to follow Lars out of the room. "It's only for one more day."

"If we even live that long."

Everyone stopped in their tracks. Slowly, they swiveled their heads to face the person responsible for saying that.

"I'm just saying what we're all thinking," Debra murmured. "The killer is still among us. Who's to say they won't start a rampage?"

"It's unlike them," Lars said curtly. "They haven't acted like that before, so we have no reason to think they'd start now. We're safe, and that's that."

"And they are still in this room. Remember that."

Lars threw up his hands in exasperation.

"If they want to kill us, they'll kill us. There is literally nothing we can do to stop that from happening. Why even worry if it's out of our control?" He smiled as all the heads in the room started nodding in agreement. "Good. Now, let's eat some dry-ass food and stop moping for one day. We're saved, damn it."

To the quarters they went. Elijah slowed down as he got up so that he and Rohan would walk out the room in unison. With everything that's been happening, he felt as though he hadn't been spending enough time with Rohan; somehow, the only times they hung out together in the submarine, it involved disposing of a dead body. That didn't leave much room for friendly banter, so Elijah didn't even try.

"Hey," he said after tapping Rohan's shoulder. "How're you holding up?"

Rohan looked slightly surprised at the inquiry, but he responded normally regardless.

"I'm tired, man. Don't get me wrong, the radio working is super cool and all . . . but really, I just feel tired."

The words struck Elijah deeply. He knew exactly what Rohan was talking about. He swallowed what felt like a gallon of air and forced himself to think of something comforting to say.

"Y'know," Elijah started, "Once we get back on the surface, maybe you'll have a chance to actually sneak up on me for once." When Rohan glanced at him with a look of confusion, Elijah hurriedly continued, "You remember the first day of training? You tried to get my bunk at some ungodly hour, and I gave you a roundhouse kick to the chin. BAM!" he said while slapping his hands together. "Just like that. And then there was the morning we found out about this whole mission. You tried to get the jump on me but ended up getting an elbow to the gut."

As he said that, he jerked his elbow out but was blocked at the last second by Rohan's hand. Genuinely shocked, he looked up to see Rohan's sunken expression brighten as he threw Elijah's arm up and forward, sending him very nearly cascading over a bunch of cardboard boxes.

After processing what just happened, Elijah picked himself up and, while laughing uproariously, smacked Rohan on the back of the head. They both continued to chuckle over the whole situation for a good minute, and when the laughter finally fell to light hiccups, Elijah spoke again.

"Just like that, man, just like that. I expect that to happen once we're back above ground."

Rohan smiled. "What I wouldn't do to breathe that musky, muddy, earthy air again."

"Careful, bud. You're beginning to sound like a normal person."

Rohan didn't reciprocate with the expected punch to the shoulder. Instead, he sighed and put his arm around Elijah.

"Thanks man," he said sincerely. "Really."

"Yeah." Elijah put his hand on Rohan's arm and shifted it off. "I know."

Chapter Twelve

Stifling Hope

If there was one thing that Elijah had learned for sure in his time in this hellhole, it was that the human body had a bizarre way of functioning. For the past three days, he had eaten nothing but packs of MREs that he washed down with dusty water. Yet, for some reason, he never ever realized he was hungry until he was opening up a new can of food. Suddenly, bellows erupted from everyone's stomachs as Lars passed around packs of food and water to everyone. From Elijah's comfortable bed, he could overhear a disagreement between Laila and Lars from across the room.

"There's only so many in there. We have to make sure we have enough to last!"

Lars scoffed in response.

"I guess you weren't listening to Arnold. We're getting out of here the day after tomorrow at the latest, so why not splurge a bit? Even if we have two MREs each today and tomorrow, there'll still be enough left to last us each another day."

"There can be delays!" Laila said in an exasperated tone. "Do you think rescuing people from the seafloor is a piece of cake? We should ration just in case."

"You can ration whatever you want," Lars grunted. "I'm having two, and I'm sure the others would like that as well."

Elijah took his pillow and folded it tightly around his ears. If walking a mile on searing-hot coals barefoot was what it took to get him some earplugs, he would do it in a heartbeat. He only stopped trying to nap when Lars tapped him on the shoulder and jiggled an MRE pack in front of him.

It was fairly subtle, but Elijah noticed how the bags became more worn and old as more days went by. He guessed that when everyone pooled the MREs from Lars' bag and the boxes in the closet, they ate the freshest packs first. Now, all that was left were questionable packets that were okay at best and foul at worst.

"Uh, Lars?" Debra called out from her bed. "I think the seal is broken on this one."

"Let me see that." He snatched it from her hand and held it up to the light in the ceiling. "Huh. Yeah, you're right." He casually tossed it back to her.

From the look on her face, Debra couldn't tell if he was joking or not. When he didn't turn to acknowledge her again, her expression became unamused.

"I'm not eating this if it's got a tear in it. Do you seriously not see the issue in that?"

Lars groaned and turned around to face her.

"Look. Mine had a small tear in it, too. If you're so worried about your food being tampered with, I'll get you something else."

"No," Debra said suddenly. "Whatever. I'm just on edge with everything going on." She waved him away. "Sorry."

"No, I'm sorry," Lars said in a much softer tone than before. "We're all a little tense, I guess. I should've known better considering what went down with . . . well, with—"

"Can you two shut up?" Rohan barked. "Some of us are trying to rest."

It was clear to Elijah, though, that he cared more about stopping Lars from saying something stupid rather than wanting the room to be silent.

After that, everyone began wolfing down their MREs. Yeah, it wasn't exactly the type of thing you'd expect from a 3-star Michelin restaurant, but food was food. Gradually, everyone's stomachs began to stop rumbling, and Elijah in particular felt like falling into a food coma. He couldn't take his pills for obvious reasons, but he figured he might as well try sleeping anyway. Before his head could even hit the pillow, however, he heard more noise coming from Debra's bed.

He turned and stared at her as she readjusted her glasses with one hand and tried to open the packet with the other.

"Do you need some help with that?"

Slightly startled, she looked up. "I got this," she insisted as she put more effort into ripping the bag open.

"Didn't you say the seal was broken on that?" Elijah inquired.

"Yeah, but that's why it's so annoying to open. The whole thing feels like it was froz—"

Before she could finish her sentence, the bag exploded under all the tension and sent bits of soup going everywhere. Debra groaned as she swiped away pieces of food from her shirt. However, instead of dwelling on the embarrassing situation, she stuck her hand into the pack and pulled out a questionable granola bar.

"Hey, isn't that supposed to be wrapped in plastic?" Rohan asked.

Debra shrugged.

"I don't care anymore. I just want to eat."

Couldn't argue with that. Elijah turned around and adjusted his blanket until it was tucked around his neck like a bib. It was mind-numbingly boring having nothing to do but eat and sleep in one room for days, but if that's what they had to do to keep everyone safe, then so be it. He could handle it.

The thing is, death didn't have to come from a person. Death could just . . . happen. And sometimes, there's nothing anyone can do to prevent it.

Abruptly, the silence was broken by a sudden intense inhale followed by several wheezing half-breaths. The sound conjured up an image in Elijah's head of a clogged vacuum cleaner sputtering on and off, over and over. When he forced himself to look over at Debra, his suspicions were proven true. She was choking on the MRE.

In an instant, both Lars and Rohan were up, scrambling across the room to try and assist her. Well, "attempt to assist her" was more accurate. Despite over a year of training in first aid, nobody could recall how to properly execute the Heimlich maneuver. While Rohan yelled instructions at Lars—who was helplessly trying to figure out what to do—Debra started squeezing her eyes shut and punching herself in the throat in a futile attempt to dislodge the culprit stealing her air. The sight was so revolting that, in any other circumstance,

Elijah would turn away in disgust and nausea. Now, after days of unrelenting desensitization to this kind of thing, he felt distant as he watched the chaos unfold.

A minute had passed. Now Laila had joined in, attempting to calm a considerably distressed Debra as both their faces turned all sorts of colorful shades. Despite everyone's best efforts, the food stubbornly remained. Amid the commotion, there was a quiet clatter as Debra's glasses slid off her nose and shattered on the ground. Then, there was a not-so-quiet scream from Rohan when he slipped while assisting Debra and cut himself on the glass from her lenses. All the while, Elijah sat upright in his bed, watching. He knew where this was going; he'd seen it too many times before.

Around the fifth round of compressions, Debra's hands stopped clawing at her neck and dropped limply to her sides. The panic and desperation in her expression gradually gave way to somber acceptance. Lars loosened his grip on her and allowed her to sway to the floor. She was still hacking relentlessly, but there was less effort in each forced exhale. She made one final attempt at a breath and stared intently at nothing as a single tear fell from her eyes. And then, she fought to speak.

"Suh . . . suh . . ."

The tears flew from her eyes exponentially faster as she gathered the will to say her final words. Finally, in tremendous pain, she spit the last thought she'd ever have.

"Suh . . . Sebastian . . ."

And with that, she croaked violently once more before going completely limp in Lars' arms. The tears had already dried from her face.

Nobody got to have the privilege of processing what just happened. Lars, hyperventilating, had already pushed Debra off of himself. In an instant, he was making a break for the door; he would've made it had Rohan not intercepted him at the last second.

"Oi!" Rohan said with his arms up like a defender in a basketball game. If his chin wasn't quivering, one would've thought he was taking the situation somewhat okay. "Where do you think you're going?" he continued.

After an unsuccessful attempt at rushing around Rohan, Lars relented.

"Look, only I can manage the radio now. The Leagues are dead, for Christ's sake! If I die, none of us are getting out of here alive. You can count on that."

"Yeah, I get that part," Rohan shouted. "But if you care so much about staying alive, why were you just running out of here alone with no warning?"

"Are you kidding?" Lars' movements became more sporadic as he fumbled over his words. "We have to tell Arnold! I knew, I goddamn knew that something was wrong with her MRE! I KNEW it, and I did NOTHING. Someone planted something in her food, and now she's dead, and it's my fault, and I have to tell Arnold or else—"

"Easy," Laila insisted. She had gotten up and was slinking over to Lars with her hand up reassuringly. "Easy. Take some deep breaths."

Her advice was lost on him. He continued rambling, "—or else I'm the reason she's dead, and I was their trainer for so long, and now they're both dead. It's my fault, and dammit, WE HAVE TO TELL ARNOLD!"

His rant had been rising in volume consistently, and now that he had finished, the room was left in silence (barring his pleading tone, which continued to echo off the walls). Finally, Elijah forced himself to hop off his bed and try to pretend that Debra's body wasn't lying limp in his peripheral vision. He approached Lars and, with some hesitation, put his hand on his shaking shoulder.

"She's not coming back." He said it bluntly, almost without emotion. "She's not coming back whether you rush to the radio now or later."

"I know you had a connection with the Leagues," Rohan added. "It must be difficult to be a mentor figure to two people and then be unable to save them. We get it."

"But you *don't.*" Lars shoved Elijah's hand away as he spoke. "You don't get it. That's the thing. If I can't save them, I can at least save us."

As this whole ordeal continued, the gears in Elijah's head began to turn. Since Sebastian's death, Lars was the only person Elijah suspected to be the killer. He knew Rohan agreed, and there was a good chance that Laila was catching on, too. And now that there were four people left . . . well, it couldn't be one of Elijah's friends. After that understanding, his attitude toward Lars shifted from empathy to apprehension.

"Why don't Rohan and I go have a look at the radio while you and Laila stay here?" he suggested.

Lars didn't hesitate. "No! I'm the only one that can control the radio! What part of this is so difficult for you to understand?"

"Well," Laila pitched in, "maybe we could—"

She was cut off by a loud grunt as Lars suddenly shoved his weight forward, toppling Rohan through the doorway. In the blink of an eye, he was halfway down the hall with Laila hot on his tail.

After recovering from the initial shock, Elijah helped a flustered Rohan up before following the two back into the control room. His feet pounded against the metal floor as he forced his brain to understand the situation. Either Lars was going through an extreme fit of psychosis, or Lars was the killer. To be fair, it would explain a lot of things, most notably the fact that he was halfway across the submarine right now. If they could catch Lars now, they could secure him until the DSRV arrived. No matter what, safety would be guaranteed then.

Elijah, still running furiously, winced as he finished that thought. After all, if he had a penny for every time he thought he was "safe" again, he'd probably have enough money to buy the submarine they was trapped in.

Approaching the control room, both Rohan and Elijah immediately analyzed the situation. Laila stood just a meter or so away from Lars, who was furiously manipulating the radio's dials and buttons while glaring threateningly in the direction of the two friends. From his theories, Elijah couldn't tell if he was truly getting it up and running—or if he was simply destroying it now that he knew no one else could fix it again.

"Lars, your hands are covered in food," Laila said admonishingly. "You really shouldn't be touching all those electronics."

He ignored her. A familiar pattern of noise erupted from the radio as Lars continued to work on it. Bits of food, water, and a negligible amount of blood flew from Lars' hands as he moved about the room. At long last, that intrusive feeling of sickness settled in Elijah's throat and stomach. Seeing this normally calm and collected man dash around the room restlessly as a way of atoning for letting someone he mentored die in his arms affected Elijah far more than watching Debra's last moments. Almost involuntarily, he stepped forward, breaching the unspoken boundary Lars had set up. He didn't care if Lars was the killer anymore; this felt too real to tolerate anymore.

"Stop it, Lars."

Lars continued to ignore him.

"I said stop it, Lars. This is getting out of hand."

Still, no luck.

Now Laila stepped in, both literally and figuratively.

"You're tampering with electrical stuff while covered in water and food, you moron. Can you slow down for one second and just wait?" She took another cautious step forward and spoke again, louder than ever. "For God's sake, at least dry your hands!"

Something about that phrase flipped a switch in Elijah's brain. He recalled a class he and Rohan had to take early on in training over how to properly handle the electronics of a military-grade computer. It was the first real "AP" lesson they got to take, so they were pretty excited. Anyway, besides learning all the jargon, there was one thing that their teacher, CDR Brookes, emphasized over and over.

"Never," she said with an expression far sterner than she ever wore normally, "under any circumstances do you touch these things with wet hands. It doesn't matter if the circuit is closed or if the wires are unexposed. If you're a fan of breathing, you'll only tamper with these with dry hands."

As Elijah's memory dispersed, his eyes subconsciously slid over to the radio itself. Lars had busted it out of the wall in order to turn it on faster, which had left some wiring exposed to the air. Laila's demands were drowned out by Elijah's own thoughts as he observed the wires. They didn't even have copper shells around them: they were just hanging around with electricity running completely uninterrupted. The same terrible feeling Elijah had in his gut when he first heard Debra wheeze was reintroducing itself, and he couldn't figure out how to stop it.

Right on cue, Lars had turned around and, with a prideful smile, finally acknowledged Laila.

"Guess what? I got it up and running while you were rambling. 'Safety' this and 'crazy' that. Y'know, Laila," he said patronizingly, "sometimes it's best to just shut up and get stuff done."

As he spoke, he began lifting the radio. He was going to affix it to the wall. The wall with at least six exposed wires ready to end his life in the blink of an eye.

"STOP!" Elijah yelled in the nick of time. Lars whirled around in confusion. After the longest second of his life, Lars relaxed his grip on the radio in frustration.

"What is it now?" he exclaimed. "What? Go on, tell me, what's so important it can't wait until after I install this thing?"

Elijah opened his mouth to tell him to put the radio down, step away, and dry his hands before he electrocutes himself. He wanted to scream at him for being so blinded by guilt that he couldn't see that he was about two seconds away from killing himself from ignorance. He wanted to say all sorts of colorful words, too.

And yet, mouth agape, he couldn't find a single thing to say in time.

Because just a second after asking the question, Lars rolled his eyes, huffed, and shoved the radio into its placement hole in the wall.

In a way, Elijah was lucky. His brain already mapped out what was coming when Lars turned away, so he instinctively threw himself to the ground, squeezed his eyes shut, and covered his ears. Laila, on the other hand, was not nearly as fortunate. Her shrieks pierced Elijah's eardrums as a frenzy of crashing sounds erupted from where Lars stood seconds ago.

His hands cupped over his ears managed to bar the uglier sounds from entering, but he could still feel the room vibrate subtly as Lars flailed around on the desk, wall, and floor. For what felt like hours, Elijah cowered there and tried to pretend he couldn't hear Laila's screeches just a foot away. After that, the thudding sounds died down, and all that was left was Laila's rapid breathlessness.

With great caution, Elijah uncurled himself and opened his eyes. His hands quickly flew from his ears to his mouth as he stifled a gag.

The sight was indescribably horrific. At least when Debra died, her face mirrored something resembling peace. Maybe she was ready to be with her brother, to escape the hell she'd been trapped in. Here, however, Lars looked like Zach after Elijah caught him with the gun over Peter's body. A vile mix of shock, fear, and stress. The sight shook Elijah so much, he didn't even realize that Rohan was behind him until a full minute later.

A jumble of nonsensical gasps exited Rohan's mouth before he managed to form a coherent thought.

"What the hell just happened?"

In response, Elijah stepped to the side and allowed Rohan to gaze upon Lars' corpse. Unlike Laila, he didn't break down into a fit of hysteria. He just stared.

"Damn."

For the next few minutes, the three of them stood around and tried to process the events that had just unfolded.

The Leagues were dead. Lars was dead. Their chance at communicating with the surface anymore was dead beyond belief. Honestly, if there was a time to throw in the towel and pray for a mercy killing, now would be the time.

Instead, Elijah began thinking. A thought was nagging him deep in the back of his brain, but it was difficult to concentrate on after all the anguish he had just sustained. Still, as he pieced it all together, he began to have a complete picture of what he really thought.

The killer was surely, absolutely, unequivocally dead. Deader than a doorknob, as his father would say. Questions had risen since the death of the commanders over who it could be, and each time they thought they had a solid grasp on the answer, another death would disprove their theory. Sebastian and Zach's simultaneous demise. The tampering in Debra's MRE. Lars' fixation on getting to the radio. Now, all of that meant nothing. The only people left on this submarine were himself and his closest friends, all of whom had alibis for every murder. It made Elijah uneasy to say, likely because he had been wrong far too many times in the past, but he felt comfortable enough to say that now . . . they were safe.

Against all odds, a chuckle escaped him. How convenient: it only took the death of nine people to guarantee their safety. Now, all they had to do was get into contact with Arnold and . . .

Oh, right.

Elijah whirled around to find his suspicions validated. Where their sole hope for rescue once stood, a charred smoking box remained instead. Without hesitation, Elijah dashed over and shook Laila and Rohan back to reality before directing them to the radio.

"Oh my god," Laila said wearily. "Oh, no. This can't be happening. Not now."

Rohan, paying no attention to how Lars' carelessness led to his electrocution, flipped the radio over absentmindedly. With a look of confusion and sorrow, he put the radio back down and looked back at his friends before shaking his head. That subtle motion dragged Elijah's spirit down lower than he'd ever known before. Slowly, he sulked over to a chair by the computers and sat down.

Laila broke the silence, evidently uncomfortable with how helpless the atmosphere was becoming.

"Well, they already have our coordinates. I heard Lars repeat it to Arnold, like, three different times. They're on their way!"

"What does it matter, though?" Rohan responded. He, too, looked like he was on the verge of tears.

"You said it yourself. What if there's a delay? What if we need to communicate with that DSRV? We're in the dark now."

As he finished saying the last sentence, the bubble in his throat finally popped, and he turned away. Obviously, in a room as painfully quiet as this one, his small sobs were deafening. His friends chose to pretend that it wasn't, however. It was the least they could do.

Finally, Laila asked the question that was weighing on everyone's minds.

"So now what?"

It was a good question.

"I wish I knew the answer," Elijah responded. "But as far as I can see, there's nothing we can do. This pile of junk—" he said while slamming his fist into the radio, causing it to crackle noisily for a moment, "—is long past fixing, even if we had the help of the Leagues or Lars. Seems like the only viable option is to wait."

"Wait for what?" Rohan questioned.

Elijah shrugged listlessly. "Just wait."

Laila nodded as the two talked, but at this statement, she picked her head up and spoke.

"And what if the DSRV isn't coming? What if we're delayed to the point that there's no more food? What if, without the radio, we can't be rescued?"

At this, Elijah held back his own rising emotions and responded expressionlessly. Honestly, everyone already knew the answer before he said it, but he chose to throw it out there anyway.

"Then it was nice to get to know you two."

He meant it.

———————

When tossing a tennis ball against the wall for hours became too tedious of a task to continue, Elijah resigned himself to counting the bumps in the ceiling for a second time. As he did, he inattentively tossed the same ball up and down with his right hand, maintaining a steady in the process. In the hours that had passed since Lars' death, this was the most exciting activity Elijah could find. He was about to reach the two-thousand marker when Rohan interrupted him.

"What is it?" Elijah asked. He had been repressing all of the events of the day, so when he spoke, he almost gave off the impression of being calm and stress-free.

Almost.

"Laila wanted me to ask you if you're sure about keeping Debra and Lars lying around in the control room," Rohan answered. "She keeps going on and on about how if the radio starts to work again or something, a bunch of rotting bodies could be a hindrance to that."

"Those rotting bodies were our friends, Rohan."

"Answer the question."

Elijah sighed and sat up, intentionally avoiding eye contact.

"Listen. I'm done. If you want to throw them in the corpse closet or keep them with Zach and Sebastian, be my guest. I'm not touching them with a ten-foot pole."

"That's the thing, though," Rohan continued. "Laila said she wouldn't do it either."

"Will you?"

The question caught Rohan a little off guard.

"Well, I mean, not if I'm the only one doing it."

"Well, there's your answer."

With that, Elijah laid back down on his bed and continued throwing and catching the ball. Annoyingly, Rohan still wouldn't leave. After a minute of uncomfortable silence, Elijah groaned and sat up again.

"Dude, what do you want?" he said, exasperated.

"Do you want to talk about everything that's happened?" The way Rohan said it made it sound like he had been rehearsing saying that same sentence for minutes before approaching Elijah. "You've been acting weird lately."

Elijah smiled coldly. "Weird, huh? Man, I wish there was some kind of explanation for that."

"You don't have to be an asshole about it," Rohan said. There was no anger in his voice, oddly enough. "I know you're on the verge, we all are. I wanted to know if you'd want to air out any of those feelings."

At this, Elijah almost laughed. "I don't know if talk therapy is going to be of much help in this scenario, bud. I appreciate the effort, though. Truly."

Rohan's unwavering stare finally broke. "Fine." He turned around and began to walk out the doorway but stopped just before the corner. Without turning around again, he said, "If you do need help, tell me. There's not much to do until we get rescued, so we might as well be there for each other."

"Noted."

When Elijah became confident that Rohan's footsteps were halfway down the submarine, he turned around to confirm that he was alone. He was. Trying to ignore the growing feeling of nausea in his gut, he went back to counting ceiling bumps.

One, two, three, four.

The feeling wouldn't go away. Elijah clenched his fists and forced himself to keep counting.

Five, six, seven, eight.

It was impossible. The rock in his throat was just moments away from escaping. But it's fine; everything's fine. He was okay.

Nine, ten, eleven.

He couldn't even make it to twelve before the downpour began. Sob after wretched sob fled his body as he silently wept into his pillow. On impulse, he screamed as loud as he possibly could into his pillow, squeezing it against his face so tightly that his knuckles began to shake. He screamed until there was no more air in his body; he screamed until he couldn't possibly grip the pillow any longer.

For a couple moments, he laid there with his face buried deep in the cushion. Perhaps he was afraid that if he looked up, Laila and Rohan would be staring at him in disgust and pity. That was ridiculous, though. He was alone.

When he lifted his face, he immediately noticed how wet the pillow was with tears and snot. If he wasn't so terribly sad, he probably would've gagged at the sight. For a minute, he took some deep breaths and composed himself. When his breathing was finally under control, he grabbed his pillow and walked over to Jacob's old bed. He switched the two, confident that nobody would be going near any of Jacob's stuff any time soon.

With his clean hand, he wiped off the tears and gunk from his face. There was no point in staying here. He couldn't go back to Rohan, though; he would immediately know what happened.

Looks like I'm paying Laila a visit.

After checking to make sure he didn't still look like a wreck, he made his way down the hall. Since everyone was confident that the killer was dead, they had enacted a new policy: do whatever the hell you want until the DSRV arrives. It was convenient, but Elijah still couldn't help but feel wary as he traversed the hallways. That was silly, though. He trusted his friends with his life. If anything, they should suspect him for the whole stint with the pills.

Elijah decided not to think further on that.

A minute later, he was outside the doorway leading into the kitchen. Inside, Laila was furiously scrubbing at the dust and grime that had been collected on the surfaces of the tables and cabinets, completely unaware of her surroundings. Elijah observed her with confusion as she continued going about her work. Why put all this effort into cleaning up a place that nobody had entered since the first day?

After realizing that watching her from the shadows was a little bit creepy, he cleared his throat loudly and stepped in. She glanced at him for a moment, smiled, and went back to wiping the table.

"Where've you been all day?"

Elijah shrugged even though she wasn't looking at him.

"Hanging out. There really isn't much to do." He took a step closer and grabbed a towel hanging by the sink. "You've just been here cleaning for hours?"

"It helps me relax," she snapped. "So, sue me."

The room fell into silence once more before Laila sighed. "Sorry."

"No, it's okay," Elijah responded. "How have you been holding up so far?"

Finally, she stopped scrubbing and looked him in the eyes.

"I'm doing alright," she admitted.

Elijah smiled and nodded in agreement, but secretly, he was hyper-focusing on her eyes. Her speech and mannerisms seemed to be normal, but her eyes looked like those of a shell-shocked soldier. It was so clear and jarring that Elijah didn't even notice that she was still speaking to him.

"Hey! Elijah!" she said louder, pulling him back to reality. "I asked: 'how're you feeling?'"

Elijah sighed and leaned against the table beside him. He thought about his encounter with Rohan and the emotional meltdown that followed. He thought about the fact that, without his pills, he wasn't getting an ounce of sleep tonight. Oh, and the fact that they were all pretending that the bodies of their friends and mentors weren't shoved in a closet somewhere. His mind raced with these thoughts as Laila patiently awaited his answer.

Finally, he opened his eyes and huffed with a small smile.

"Honestly? Never felt better."

CHAPTER THIRTEEN

OUTTA LUCK

A while back, Elijah read up on something known as "Chinese water torture" for a school psychology project. It was an incredibly fascinating phenomenon wherein a prisoner would be bound to the point that any meaningful movement was impossible. Then, once they were fully aware of their surroundings, a bucket would leak a drop of ice-cold water onto their head or face at random intervals. As the minutes ticked into hours, the irregular drops of water would cause the prisoner to go completely insane as every moment became one of dread and anticipation for the next drop. Elijah remembered delivering a kick-ass presentation on it at school the day after reading about it, too. And now, funnily enough, he was the victim.

Just as he completed that thought, the radio whirred obnoxiously for the sixth time in a row. Elijah, once again, was caught off guard and threw his pen across the room reflexively. Sighing, he stood to go over and pick it up, glaring at the radio as he did so. It was tragically ironic, really: the object that had been their symbol of hope in bleak times was now a hindrance to Elijah's writing. After taking a deep breath to compose himself, he got back to it.

In the time since he and Laila cleaned up the entire kitchen, the list of productive things to do in the submarine dwindled faster and faster. Rohan and Laila resigned themselves to taking multiple naps throughout the day to pass time, something that Elijah was furiously envious of. He only had one pill left, and he was prepared to save it for when he truly needed it. The downside, of course, being that he had to find something to do while his friends dozed peacefully.

Finding nothing better to do, Elijah decided to rest in the control room (*Huh, Rohan moved Lars to a closet after all!*) and write down his experiences in the submarine so far. He was never much of a writer—the only times he ever got Bs in school were in English classes—but he decided to try journaling regardless to conserve his sanity. If it weren't for the radio acting up every couple of minutes, Elijah could've written without hassle. Instead, he tensed up as the minutes ticked by, anticipating the next burst of noise to interrupt him yet again.

It was a waste of time to worry about; he had to get back to work. Deciding to start at the beginning, he scribbled details of the look on Patrick's face when Rohan came barging into the room for the informational meeting back on the surface. He wrote about the ecstatic conversations he and his friends shared at mess hall afterward and the squabbles that seemed oh-so-important back then. He wrote about the indescribable feeling of climbing down the hatch of a submarine for the first time and feeling the cool metal floor beneath him.

He wrote about finding the bodies of his mentors barely a day after the mission began.

WHIRRRR! WHIRRRR! WHIRRRR!

This time, Elijah held onto his pen. In fact, he barely even reacted to the radio. He was too lost in his own thoughts to recognize anything going on in the physical space around him. When he did come to, he put the pen down and walked over to the radio calmly. He observed it for a moment before slamming his fist into it with incredible force. The box whined in response, but the whirring seemed to quiet down, if only for a moment, before ceasing completely. Elijah returned to his seat.

In the coming hours, Elijah did nothing but write and crack his knuckles intermittently. He was so absorbed in it, he hardly noticed that the radio was silent for the rest of the day. The only time he paused was when his pen ran out of ink, and he was forced to dash to the supply closet to grab another. Word after word, paragraph after paragraph, he constructed a novella containing his experiences. The few but meaningful highs. The unspeakably deep lows. Zach. His friends. His house back in New Mexico. It was all here, organized in a single fluent session.

When he finished, Elijah sat up and rubbed his eyes, feeling the weight of the ache of exhaustion finally begin to crush him. He had managed to stave it off for a while by sheer will, but even that wouldn't save him now. Groggily, he dragged himself out of the control room and into the hallway, half-considering just laying down on the cool metal floor and napping there. Instead, he gritted his teeth and continued. He got to the quarters soon after and slinked into his bed, head lolling about like a bowling ball attached to a stick.

"You doing alright?" Laila asked from across the room.

Elijah didn't even notice that she was there when he crawled in.

"Yeah," he said. "Just tired."

Laila nodded in response. "Do you have any idea where Rohan is?"

"Laila, I'm not even completely sure I know where I am right now."

That miserable attempt at a joke actually got a chuckle out of her.

"I get that, man," she said reassuringly.

The way she spoke made it sound like they were just having a normal conversation the way they did back on the surface. It was nice, and it made Elijah want to smile, if only his facial muscles would obey.

"Hey, where's Rohan, anyway?" she asked.

Elijah shrugged.

"Well, I just got here, and I assumed he was with you. You're saying he wasn't?"

"Nope," Elijah responded while fluffing up his pillow.

"Hmm." There was silence as they both pondered that understanding.

"That's odd," she said finally. "I feel like we should go check on him just in case."

"What for?" Elijah murmured. "There's no murderer anymore. He's probably fine."

"Yeah." Laila hesitated. "Maybe you're right. I guess I'm just on edge with everything else that's been going on."

"Rest," Elijah said. "We'll all feel better after that. Then, we'll meet up with Rohan and eat some good-old-fashioned MREs and wait for the DSRV to get here."

"Yeah. You're right." Her voice was unconvincingly calm. "See you in the morning, Elijah."

"Mmhmm," Elijah muttered as he forced the last pill down his dry throat and gulped harshly. It felt like it was tearing at the sides of his esophagus as it traveled down. Were Elijah slightly more aware, he might've seen how stupid that action was. Everyone had already demonstrated their incompetence at helping a choking person, and here he was not having water with his pills out of sheer laziness.

As he sat there in silence, trying to ignore the deep gnawing sensation in his throat, he thought about all that had happened recently. If everything went according to schedule (and there was no indication that it wouldn't), then he, Rohan, and Laila were free tomorrow evening. He had every thought put down on paper in the control room, and when they finally got to the surface, they could finally identify who it was that caused so many innocent people to die. Yep. Everything would be fine.

When Elijah thought it this time, he truly believed it. Everything would be fine. For the first time in a while, he genuinely smiled as his head melted into the pillow. Somewhere else in the room, Laila was already snoring softly. It felt safe in a strange way. It felt like home.

His last thought before he drifted off to sleep was what Rohan could be doing right now.

Honestly, whatever it is, I guarantee it's not as relaxing as this.

––––––––

When Elijah came to, he was so groggy that he was certain he was dreaming. After rubbing his eyes, he flexed his entire body and pinched himself to make sure that he was truly awake. When that was confirmed, he forced himself to step out of bed and ignore how warm his sheets were in comparison to the frigid air. Bone cracking noises enveloped the room as he stretched his shoulders and legs.

"Good morning," he said aloud to himself with a smile.

Even while thousands of feet deep in the ocean, he felt like he could taste the sunlight on his face. He could barely contain his excitement to feel the grass between his toes back on the surface as he ran down the hallway. He turned excitedly, hoping to see his friends share this sentiment, only to find that Laila was fast asleep, and Rohan was nowhere to be seen.

That's odd, he thought to himself. *He must've gotten up before us, then.*

It was the only explanation, unless Rohan had decided to sleep on the floor of whatever room he was in before. Elijah chuckled softly. Knowing Rohan, Elijah wouldn't put it past him.

After double-checking to make sure Laila was still asleep, Elijah quickly got changed and shoved his old clothes into his pack before heading out the door. He wasn't worried about Rohan enough to go on a search just yet; he was more interested in finishing his journal. Now would be a good time to name it. "Life in the Death Submarine" had an okay ring to it, but frankly, he knew he could do much better than that.

As he approached the control room, his ears picked up a familiar voice. A sly grin spread on his face as he began to think of a plan. He paused, planting his foot on the door to the control room with precision. Then, after waiting for a moment, he kicked it in as hard as he could, running in with his arms up threateningly like a leopard about to pounce. As expected, Rohan flew up from his chair and screeched in terror momentarily before realizing that he was the victim of a crude prank. Irritated, he shoved Elijah away while breathing deeply to calm himself down. Elijah, too, was struggling to maintain his composure, although in this case, it was from laughter, not fright.

"You and I both know why that wasn't funny," Rohan said. Despite his best attempts, his suppressed smile was shining through.

Elijah smirked and put his hands up defensively.

"Aw, come on," he responded. "It was funny for me. That's all that really matters at the end of the day."

Rohan didn't even bother replying. He simply rolled his eyes and walked over to where he sat earlier. The floor was now covered in loose paper and notes. Elijah squinted closer and saw his name quickly scribbled over the top of every page.

"Were you reading my stuff?" he questioned.

Rohan looked slightly taken aback.

"Well, I mean, it was all right here for anyone to read. I didn't think you'd want your diary to be a secret if it would just be out in the open."

"Hey," Elijah said reassuringly. "Quit being so defensive. I don't have an issue with it."

Then, out of the blue, he smacked Rohan on the side of the head.

"Don't call it a diary, though, unless you want some more of that."

Rohan laughed and faked a lunge at Elijah, causing him to step back and falter for a moment. Grinning, Elijah stooped down and began picking up the papers.

"Where were you all of yesterday, anyway?

"What do you mean?" His eyebrows creased in confusion. "I was in the room down the right hallway counting up the food. I found a reclining chair there, too, so I decided to sit down."

"Let me guess," Elijah groaned, "you fell asleep there."

Rohan shrugged, prompting Elijah to roll his eyes. At that moment, he had gathered up all of the papers and was sorting them into the correct order. As he tried to ignore his awful handwriting, he began to wonder what Rohan thought of everything he had scribbled down. Then, almost as if he could read his mind, Rohan spoke.

"It isn't bad," he admitted. "The book, I mean."

"Calling it a book is ambitious," Elijah responded. "But thanks. I figure once we get back on the surface, it'll be good for everyone to have a timeline of what went down here day by day while it's still fresh in my mind."

Rohan looked back at the papers inquisitively.

"Oh," he said stupidly. "I thought you were going to sell copies and make a bunch of money off of this mess."

"Come on, dude," Elijah said sarcastically. "That comes after."

The two chuckled, then fell into silence as Rohan read some pages over Elijah's shoulder. It felt natural, standing together like that; it almost felt like they were back on the surface in the dorm rooms, with Rohan yapping at Elijah upside down from the top bunk about some meaningless topic. Elijah smiled. Words couldn't express how excited he was to return to normalcy again.

The smile quickly dropped from Elijah's face as he contemplated that. Up until now, he had been selling himself the lie that, once the killer was caught and they were back on land, things would return exactly to how they were before. He'd quit the Navy and go back to New Mexico. He'd still meet up with Laila every now and then, and he'd stay in touch with Rohan. Now, with that reality becoming ever more likely, he was forced to grapple with the very real possibility that that wouldn't happen. Of course, there'd be an investigation into everything that had happened. He'd be questioned, day-in and day-out on his dead friends, mentors, and allies. He'd never again catch a glimpse of Lars beaming proudly at Sebastian and Debra as they worked on a radar system. He'd never again roll his eyes at an ignorant comment by Cassidy. He'd never again feel as tiny as an insect under Patrick's tough gaze.

No, he thought. *Nothing's ever going to be like it was before.*

The realization weighed his head down and caused his shoulders to droop. Still, if there was one thing that wasn't going away, it was his friends. As long as they were breathing, Elijah could find a way to manage.

"Hey." Rohan had a concerned look on his face. "You okay?"

Elijah blinked a couple times and took a deep breath, before turning to Rohan.

"Yeah, man. Just thinking about some things."

"Aren't we all," Rohan said grimly.

Before another awkward silence could spring up, Elijah sat down and pulled out a pen from his pants pocket while resting some blank papers on his lap.

"I think I'm going to stay here and write some more," he announced without looking up at Rohan. "If you want to stay, feel free. I just thought of some more stuff I need to jot down."

"I don't want to intrude," Rohan started while backing away.

"That's a first. Hey, I'm just kidding!" Elijah said while laughing at Rohan's offended face.

"I'll probably go prepare some of our crewmates' bags so that they're ready to be transported up, then," Rohan decided.

"How selfless," Elijah said soberly, "but Laila's sleeping right now. How about we all do that in an hour or so? Maybe we could hold a little remembrance type of thing for them, too."

Rohan thought deeply about that proposition and nodded.

"Sure. I guess I'll just count the MREs we have left, then."

"Alright." Elijah turned back to his papers. "Good luck with that."

The door swung shut behind Rohan as he left, leaving Elijah in complete solitude to begin writing. Still, even after five minutes of being left alone, he couldn't help but spin his pencil around his fingers aimlessly while staring off into nothing. Despite an earnest effort, his mind was being annoyingly uncooperative, and the more he sat there with paper strewn across his lap, the more daunting it felt to begin writing.

A few more minutes of this went on before Elijah finally snapped out of it. In a brief moment of clarity, he cursed his brain fog and started writing down the incoherent thoughts that were going on in his mind without regard for sense or readability. He started with talking about how much he missed his parents despite their flaws, which evolved into him sharing his utter bafflement that a submarine would only have one functional radio. Shortly thereafter, he began questioning why any self-respecting parent would name their daughter "Cassidy," which loosely transitioned into a rant on the spelling and pronunciation of the word "psychology."

In reality, Elijah knew that what he was scribbling was complete gibberish. But as his hand flew across the pages, spilling these incomprehensible ideas, memories, and feelings, he found that he couldn't bring himself to stop. It was—put simply—cathartic. At long last, when he had finally exhausted the pen to the point that no amount of pressure would release another droplet of ink, he slumped back into the chair he sat in and gasped for breath. What he had written was nothing like the methodically planned-out sequence of events he wrote the day prior—that's for sure—but he felt the weight on his chest had shrunk slightly. The overwhelming flood of emotions in the quarters yesterday seemed like a distant memory, perhaps even a figment of the imagination. He stood, steadying himself so as to not fall over, and observed the mess of sheets that lay around him.

Maybe I should just quit the Navy and become a philosopher, he thought to himself. Ah, who was he kidding. Philosophers were actually smart.

As he bent down to pick up the papers (for the second time in an hour, bizarrely), his mind began to wander. He thought about what he would say to his parents when they would inevitably receive him on the shore. Would he show them what he wrote? Probably not, there was a little too much carnage and terror in there for any sane person to read without feeling the urge to throw up. Hell, it might traumatize them more than it did him.

Whatever the case, he would be glad—no, thrilled—to see them. The cycle of waking up, initially oblivious to his surroundings, only to have his heart jump to his throat as he realized that he and his friends could die at any moment was all too much to bear. Tears started to well up in his eyes, and unlike yesterday, he let them flow freely. He slowly began to realize that, more than anything, he needed to get away from it all. He wanted to close his eyes, clench his fists, and open them back up to see the faces of his parents, the doorway to his home, or anything that wasn't the monotonous hellish gray of the interior of this submarine.

A few more hours, he reminded himself. *Just hold out for a few more hours.*

At that precise moment, picking up the last page that he had dropped, he heard a fit of rustling just outside the door. Taken aback at first, he smiled after realizing who it must be.

"You can't scare me, Laila!" he laughed from behind the door. "You're not nearly sneaky enough."

His smirk wavered slightly when he received no response.

"You can come in anyway. I've been working on something that I want to show you."

Still, no response.

Now, Elijah's expression of glee was nonexistent.

That's odd, he thought. That noise sounded unnaturally muffled, almost as if he was listening to music with headphones that had recently been dropped in a glass of water. If this was still someone's attempt at scaring him, it was getting gradually more effective.

He was about to speak again when he heard another sound so unbelievably quiet, he couldn't be sure he had heard it at all. It was the sound of raspy breathing followed by tiny clicks, like the sound a bicycle makes when you change the gear.

Elijah, still sitting perfectly still, listened closer. The terrifying realization that he probably wasn't being pranked sunk in. Frozen like a deer in the headlights, he tried to gulp for air as his heartbeat soared and his mind raced.

Could it be happening all over again?

That's ridiculous, he thought. *You're overreacting.*

And you know what? Maybe he was.

Had he not written about how jittery and uptight his experiences in the submarine had made him? Had he not admitted to himself that, unequivocally, they were safe? Laila was asleep. Rohan was off somewhere counting MREs. What the hell was Elijah thinking?

It was difficult to do, but Elijah managed to center himself back to reality and calm down. It was fine. He was safe. Rescue was on the way. Like a religious mantra, he repeated these phrases to himself until finally, finally his heart began to beat normally again. God, that was silly. Who knew some rustling plastic could get that great of a reaction out of him?

"Jesus," he sighed aloud to no one in particular. "I need to get a grip on myself."

Then, he heard something shatter.

He was out the door before his brain could even register what was happening. He felt exactly like he did when Zach fired the gun a few days ago: zero cognitive processes, only an unstoppable urge to get to the source of the sound. He was screaming, but he couldn't even hear what he was saying. He was flying around the hall, trying every door, slamming every lock, until he finally determined that the noise had to have come from the closet.

Now he was fully aware of his surroundings. Filled with immeasurable momentum, he backed up slowly and deliberately, like an assassin slinking back into the shadows after a kill. Then, with a yell capable of shattering a wine glass, he threw himself at the door shoulder-first, causing it to slam open and send him crashing into the floor. He was so high on adrenaline, he hardly noticed that the door was unlocked, and that his ridiculous maneuver was unnecessary.

The noise was getting louder now. Unmistakably, someone was gasping for air on the other side of the door. This time, maintaining a smidge of composure, Elijah tried the door handle. It didn't work.

"Hold on!" he pleaded to the mystery victim on the other side of the door. "I'm coming, just please, hold on!"

The response was a chaotic clammer of falling boxes and objects from the other side.

Goddamnit, Elijah thought to himself as he rubbed his wounded shoulder. He winced as he tapped it, revealing his inability to break down another door without seriously injuring himself. That door wouldn't budge.

No, no, no, no . . .

The breathing was slowing on the other side. What was once a desperate call for help had withered down to a series of intermittent squeals of pain. If anything, this only made Elijah's brain race for solutions faster, and he began tearing up the room in search of something to pry the door open with. He emptied shelf after shelf and box after box, sending screwdrivers, tissue boxes, and random tech flying over his shoulder as he did so. Finally, deciding that time was of the essence, he grabbed a hammer from the bottom of a box he had thrown before and walked over to the door.

Pushing the pathetic whimpering out of his mind, he lifted the hammer up over his head and struck the area between the knob and the lock underneath. In response, a ringing noise echoed quietly on the other side, similar to the noise of a coin spun on a countertop. Deciding to scream for energy this time, Elijah once again struck the knob with the hammer, causing the noise from before to grow louder in protest. He listened closely to see if he had made any progress, only to realize that there was no more clamor coming from the other side. He couldn't even hear any breathing anymore.

If he was getting in, he had to get in now.

Looking at the door before him, he felt small. He knew that there was only one shot of getting in, and worse, he knew what it would cost. Still, what other choice did he have? There was somebody that needed his help just a few feet away from him. He couldn't just leave them for dead. Now, he didn't care who that person was, how they were alive, or how they ended up in that position. All he cared about was getting in.

He stepped back, massaging his right shoulder as he did. A countdown timer had already begun in his head. His fists folded up tightly, displacing the sweat that had been collecting on his palms.

Before closing his eyes, he took one slow careful look at the door, the barrier that was keeping him from saving the person on the other side. Then, he shifted his feet to get a running start and, without faltering, sprinted and threw his wounded shoulder directly into the wall.

Elijah thought he knew pain, but he was sorely mistaken. What he was feeling now . . . well, put simply, no language ever created could adequately describe the fire working its way up his arm. Even so, the torture was momentarily suspended by the realization that the door had budged slightly. He kicked the door in now, wincing as the pressure echoed into his arm, and collapsed inside, eyes frantic in search of the victim. Instead, all he found were several MREs scattered around the floor from the impact he made with the door, as well as a few on the many shelves around him. He had never seen this room, but now that he had, he assumed that this was where all of the food had been kept for so long.

That revelation wasn't important in the moment, however; he had just laid eyes on what looked like an unmoving body. Instinctively, he put his arm on the floor to lift himself up, but immediately regretted the decision as his arm collapsed in yet another wave of inarticulable pain.

Damn it, he thought helplessly. *Please, please don't be dead.*

Opting to crawl on the floor like a worm (still painful, but not nearly as much as before), he almost fell flat on his face once he got a better look at the person. A plastic bag had been zip-tied onto their head so tightly that they couldn't breathe, and their hands and feet were bound together through the same method as well. Their face was grinding against the ground, and their arms and legs were tied behind their back to the point that they looked like cattle in a meat-processing factory. It was a repulsive sight, but Elijah didn't care. He kept pushing forward, inch by inch, until he got a good look at the victim's face.

Up until this point, Elijah had simply ignored the thoughts he had had since he first heard the scream.

Was it a trap? Who could it be? Is the killer back?

Those questions, although critically important, seemed irrelevant to him when it was clear that someone was in danger. Now, after the adrenaline had dipped and he had successfully breached the door, it began to dawn on him that there were only two people that could possibly be asphyxiating in that bag. And now, he was staring into the unseeing eyes of one of them.

"Rohan."

Time stood still; all sound ceased. The only thing that was real in that moment was Rohan's petrified unmoving face, staring right back at him.

"Rohan?"

It had to be a joke, right? Some kind of elaborate prank? But then . . . why were there so many MREs laying about? Was this where he had been getting all of the food for so long? And why was the inside of the bag covered in condensation and spit and . . .

Suddenly, it didn't matter. None of it mattered. All that mattered was getting him out of that bag. He wailed noiselessly as he lifted his broken shoulder to claw a hole through the plastic, scratching and tearing desperately at the resistant surface.

"ROHAN!" he screeched as he slashed at the bag, flipping Rohan's limp neck over and around as he did so. He screamed his name again, and as he did, he finally managed to tear a hole with his bloodied chipped fingernails. Without delay, he reached both hands into the tiny hole and ripped it off, involuntarily tightening the zip-ties around Rohan's neck. Tears collected on the torn bag. It took him a moment to realize they were his.

The bag eventually came off of Rohan's head, but they still weren't out of the woods yet.

Damn it, Elijah cursed. Just as he did a thousand times over in basic training, he flipped Rohan over, slid the zip-ties down his wrists, and put his arms sturdily over Rohan's chest to perform CPR.

This was it. He was going to make it. He had to, after all. This wasn't the first time Elijah had done CPR, and dammit, it wouldn't be the last. He took a deep breath and, with will unmatched, he pushed down to do a compression. That's when the dam finally broke.

The second the compression began, Elijah knew. He felt it, not just in his arm or shoulder, but in the very core of his being. He knew before his nervous system could tell his brain what was happening. He knew before the pain even began. He knew that, no matter how determined he was, no matter how much strength he could summon . . . he couldn't do it.

And then, the wave finally crashed over him. He had been swimming a mile upstream this whole time, fighting fiercely to maintain his momentum, to not stop until he had saved his friend. And yes, it worked for a time. But now, no amount of kicking or thrashing or flailing would work. He gave into the pain and fell back helplessly onto a box of MREs, wallowing in torment as everything collapsed.

Elijah had never felt a sensation similar to this before. He knew pain so terrible that it could make you scream and roar in agony, so horrible that it could make you wish you were dead. But this. This was different. It was as if his brain had forbade him from doing anything that would bring him further harm. He had, metaphorically, been switched off. The only action he could muster was to shake and quiver in a chorus of pathetic sobs as he looked his dying friend in the eyes, fully aware of how close he was to saving him.

It may have been a figment of Elijah's imagination, but he swore he saw Rohan's lips move one final time. At this point, his psyche was so messed up that everything he was seeing could've been a lie, but he didn't care. In his pitiful, childlike, miserable state, he could've sworn that Rohan attempted to mouth the words "thank you" to him. Whether he had imagined it or not, it was too much. He closed his eyes and buried his face in the box beside him.

There was nothing more to be done. He had failed, and now Rohan was dead.

Who did this? He thought to himself. *How? Why is this still happening?*

He did not know, and frankly, he didn't care to find out anymore. The seconds ticked by as he waited for sensation to return to his arm. If he was being completely truthful with himself, he wouldn't mind dying right there and then. He couldn't fathom ever getting up from where he was now, going on with life, and pretending that he wasn't broken beyond repair. In fact, he didn't think anything could give him the will to sit up again.

And then, there was a noise in the hall. Footsteps. Slow, deliberate, careful footsteps approaching from the same route Elijah had used to enter. Boxes clattered to the side and glass crunched underneath an invisible foot as the unknown person crossed that hall.

Against all odds, Elijah felt his heartbeat and breathing begin to rise in intensity. He already knew who it was before they even came into sight.

His back straightened as he recognized her.

"Laila."

It was her. Hands flat at her sides in pure shock, hair disheveled like she had just woken up, and eyes locked on Rohan's contorted body.

"Laila," he gasped with force. "I tried. I really did. I couldn't do it." The tears streaming down his face accelerated and began to dampen the box he laid on. "It was too late. Please, Laila, I did everything I could."

She didn't even look at him. She just continued to stare at Rohan, carefully observing the zip-ties and torn bag and pained expression on his face. Then, only after taking in as much of the scene as she could, she turned to a panicked Elijah.

"We're not safe," Elijah spit out before wincing in agony as his arm moved slightly off the box. "Someone did this to Rohan, and they're going to do it to us."

She's still not speaking. Why won't she say anything? Why is she just standing there expressionless, like this is an everyday occurrence to her?

"Laila." It was getting harder to speak by the minute. "I can't move. I need help. Please, before that person comes back and does the same thing to us."

"They won't."

Her expression had changed. Her eyebrows rose, and she stretched her arms out to the side casually, but underneath that calm demeanor, Elijah could tell she was in distress.

"I know who the killer is."

Elijah's arm almost fell off the box in shock at that statement, sending another wave of searing pain up his arm.

"Who? Tell me who, please!"

Just as he finished that sentence, an object in Laila's pocket caught the light and struck Elijah square in the eyes. His eyes squinted to avoid the glare, but they quickly widened as he realized what it was.

Laila wiped a tear off her face, reached behind her pocket, and, with a trembling hand, pulled out a gun.

Zach's gun.

She shut her eyes tight as she lifted it to aim between Elijah's eyes, hand shaking more than ever now. She was losing her composure, but she held on long enough to say a single sentence.

"Elijah," she said aggressively, "it's time for you to confess."

Chapter Fourteen

The Confession

Suddenly, Elijah wasn't thinking about the DSRV, his arm, or even Rohan anymore. All he could focus on was the barrel of the gun that was pointed square at his nose.

"What?"

"You heard me," she repeated. "Confess."

"Confess what?" He may have been still as a statue from shock, but his voice quivered more than the gun did in Laila's hands.

"Shut UP!" Laila commanded. "For the love of god, please, just stop pretending. Don't you owe me—don't you owe US—that much?"

Slowly, Elijah moved his arm to grab onto the ledge beside him. He felt like he was being raided by the FBI. One wrong move, and the barrel of that gun would be the last thing he'd ever lay his eyes on.

"Laila," he stuttered, "are you saying that I did those things to our friends?" His fright very briefly gave way to anger. "To Rohan? You think I could do something like that?"

"It's not about thinking," she said coldly. "I know. I've been watching you since Zach was shot. I know you're behind all this."

Elijah opened his mouth to speak but was met with a thunderous smash as Laila knocked a box of MREs onto the ground.

"Enough!" she said, unhinged. "Look me in the eye and tell me the truth!"

How is this happening? Elijah thought. It didn't make any sense. She had known him for longer than everyone else on the submarine, and she genuinely thought he could be the culprit? This had to be a mistake; it was the only explanation for her pointing a gun at his head so confidently.

"Okay," Elijah responded calmly, "let's take a deep breath now. Don't do anything that you'll regret for the rest of your life."

Her grip on the trigger loosened. Good.

"First things first," Elijah said. "Where'd you get the gun?"

"It's Zach's." She shook her head like it was obvious. "I grabbed it from beneath my bed when I heard all that commotion. Yeah," she replied to Elijah's confused face, "I've held onto it for safety since Lars got zapped. Sue me."

"Okay. Why exactly do you think I'm the killer?" he asked earnestly. He wasn't even trying to distract her. He really was curious as to why she suspected him so much.

"We're the last two people left," she said bluntly. "I'm not the killer, so it has to be you."

Elijah forced his arm to remain still, even as another wave of pain traveled through it.

"Okay," he started. "Do you have any other reasons besides that? Or are you going to murder your best friend of the better part of a decade over some rudimentary process of elimination?"

"I don't know what that means."

Elijah sighed. If his life wasn't in mortal peril, he'd probably assume this was all some big joke.

"I do know this, though. You're an insomniac. You have been since the day I met you. So, I just find it funny that, with you being the only person who can reliably stay up all night, most of the killings happen during nighttime."

"Oh, come *on*," Elijah groaned, genuinely vexed from what he was hearing. "You know about the pills. I've slept alongside you guys every night, full stop."

At that, Laila began to smirk.

"Funny you should mention pills. You want to explain to me how Lars found them on Zach after YOU searched him?"

Damn it. She had a point.

"I honestly don't know," he lamented. "Really."

"Oh, don't worry. I have a pretty good idea of how that could've happened." She readjusted her aim, her grip sturdier than before.

"And what about Sebastian? There's only one person I know that can sneak through the dead of night so quietly that they wake no one."

"I know you don't hear yourself talking right now," Elijah said, "because you are making some of the most insane reaches I have ever heard in my entire life. Do you have any evidence that isn't tied together by a thread?"

"I don't know about that," Laila growled. "I'd say the pills being on Zach is pretty damning. You could've worked with someone to take care of Peter. I'll figure out the details later, but right now, I know in my heart that you had something to do with this." Her teeth gnashed as she tried to hide her fury. "I can't believe you."

It suddenly dawned on Elijah that Laila wasn't acting hysterical. The more he looked at the situation from an objective lens, the more he realized that she was right: it *did* look like he was orchestrating all of this. The very thought caused him to shake.

"Laila," he began, but he couldn't continue. Out of nowhere, his shoulder began wailing in pain, and he tumbled to the floor in a fit of suffering. His repressed screams still managed to escape his mouth, and although his mind was primarily occupied by the agony he was in, he was self-aware enough to know he looked pathetic right now.

"Why do all this, Elijah?" Laila was crying now, silent tears streaming down her face as her grip on the gun tightened. "Why do any of this?"

"Okay," Elijah hissed through clenched teeth, "you got me. I killed them all. Let's pretend I don't have an alibi for half the deaths, let's pretend you haven't known me for half of your life, and let's pretend that I have a motive for any of this." With great effort, he twisted his neck to look her in the eyes. "How would shooting me now solve any of that?"

Laila looked genuinely shocked at that comment.

"I'm not going to shoot you, idiot."

"Then do me a favor," he seethed, "and get that goddamn gun out of my face."

He could see the will beginning to wear down in Laila's eyes. Her shoulders began to slump forward, her head swayed to the side, and her eyes declared her mental exhaustion. The gun, however, remained exactly where it was.

"Your pills were on Zach. You were the one who found the MREs that Debra choked on. And now, you're the one who found Rohan," her voice began to quake with anger. "Rohan, dammit! Tell me something, Elijah. If you didn't do this, who did?"

"How could I have done it?" Elijah wanted to scream. "I have a broken shoulder, you asshole! You think I can wrestle a guy like Rohan to the ground when I can't even move my own arm?" He chuckled in disbelief. "You're insane."

She didn't even react.

"Who killed him then, Elijah?"

His smile waned. She was right about that. This wasn't the type of thing to happen by accident, and both he and Laila had an alibi. But . . . who else could've done it, then?

"Ah." She frowned in disgust. "Now look who's quiet."

The more this conversation went on, the more Elijah felt like there would be no positive outcome.

"Laila, listen. The DSRV should be here soon. We can both get on, get up to the surface, and you can spill your suspicions to whoever the hell you want. But please," he forced his voice to sound earnest, "you don't want to do this."

He meant every word he was saying, but truthfully, he was really trying to get her to lower her guard. The second her gun was pointed away from his head, he was going to do one final tackle and secure it for himself.

It's risky, he thought, but it's less risky compared to having a hysterical person pointing at me for hours. One thoughtless slip-up on her part, and he'd join Rohan.

"Don't move," she ordered. Any progress that had been made earlier was stalemated now: Laila wasn't budging. "If we have to stand like this for two more hours, so be it. I won't make another fatal mistake."

Emotions continued to cloud Elijah's mind. It was all too much: watching one friend die just for another to turn on him, the possibility that the DSRV would never arrive, and the brutality of Rohan's death. He wanted so much to scream until his vocal chords were torn beyond repair, but his exhaustion wouldn't permit it. Instead, he just mumbled under his breath as he slumped against the box behind him.

"I'm tired."

Just as he predicted, Laila faltered. His opportunity was opening up by the second.

"I am too," Laila responded, unaware of the fact that her guard was falling.

Elijah gritted his teeth and shifted off the box. The pain hadn't diminished one bit, but he managed to push it out of his head long enough to sneak a foot out underneath his hip. His heart raced as he realized what he was about to do. Every second counted. If there was ever a time to focus on the task at hand, it was now.

Laila's gaze was refocusing. In an instant, her absent-mindedness would return to feverish defense, and Elijah would be stuck again.

He took a breath. He relaxed his shoulder. He said a quick prayer for himself, Rohan, and all the others.

Then, before Laila could even move her finger back to the trigger, he had leapt into the air like a starving cougar, tackling Laila to the ground. A gunshot went off. It missed.

This wasn't the friendly type of scuffling middle-schoolers do on the playground when someone loses the kickball. This was a violent mess of shrieks, punches, and elbows to the face. With his functional arm, Elijah clocked Laila in the jaw before swiveling around and reaching for the gun. Wearing a facial expression mixed with shock and unadulterated hatred, she slammed down on his knee before he could get to it in time. Luckily for Elijah, the adrenaline coursing through his veins made it so his ears couldn't pick up on the frequency he was screaming at. Otherwise, he may have gone deaf.

Laila had just about secured the gun before Elijah pulled her leg out from underneath, sending her crashing down into the boxes beside her. A thick THWANG noise erupted as her head slammed into the metal bar of the cabinet beside her. She spent no less than a second dwelling on the pain before lunging back at Elijah.

"I KNEW IT!" she yelled as she clawed at Elijah's face and hands, attempting to disarm him. "YOU BASTARD! HOW COULD YOU? HOW—" she elbowed him in the nose, "COULD—" she lifted his broken shoulder and slammed it into the same bar she had fallen on, "YOU?"

Her fist was raised in preparation for another round of beatings before she composed herself and sat down instead, gun in hand. For a few moments, Elijah didn't move. He was having too much trouble breathing to do so. Every time he attempted a shaky inhale, the blood pouring from his nose and forehead was inhaled as well, sending him into coughing fit after coughing fit. His vision was obscured by a single streak of blood dripping from his brow, but it didn't matter anyway: one of his eyes was too blurry to make out anything farther than a foot away. He was, however, able to notice Laila's condition. Blood streaked down her nose as well, and her hair barely covered the massive bruise on her jaw that Elijah had delivered. Also, she was swaying where she stood, evidently shook by the head trauma she had sustained.

"Damn it," she seethed under her breath as she wavered in place. "I can't believe you. Have you always been like this? Did I ever even know you?"

Elijah didn't respond. He knew that, after doing something that insane, he had absolutely no way of defending his innocence anymore. Instead, he flopped over and gasped for air haphazardly. Every atom in his body was squealing in agony—at least, the parts of his body he could feel. The realization that he couldn't feel anything from the waist down was far more terrifying than any tangible pain could ever be.

Even so, Elijah racked his brain for a last-ditch plan he could execute. If he gave up now, everyone on the surface would believe without a doubt that he was the killer. Why wouldn't they? With that idiotic attack, he had basically given any prosecutor the ammunition they needed to put him away indefinitely. More than anything, the thought of Laila, his family, and everyone he'd ever met believing that he murdered those people in cold blood, that he'd murdered Rohan . . . he couldn't stomach it.

As his mind raced, he began to notice the feeling in his throat shift. With a quick glance, he noticed that Laila was still stabilizing herself on the wall, trying to recover mentally from the strike to her head. Slowly, one final Hail Mary idea began to hatch in Elijah's mind. If it worked, he'd guarantee his safety until the DSRV arrived. If unsuccessful . . . well, things couldn't get much worse anyway.

Cautiously, Elijah forced out a cough. It made his temples and throat sear with pain, but after the hacking fit he had just endured a minute or two ago, he could more than handle it. Laila didn't even bat an eye. She just kept wheezing and massaging her head on the opposite side of the room.

Good, Elijah thought. *Now, I've got to lose the subtlety.*

After bracing himself, Elijah forced out another wave of coughs and other disgusting noises, so much so that he began to cough for real as a reflex. Out of the corner of his eye, he could barely make out Laila beginning to turn in his direction. He forced the chorus of hiccups and coughs to continue through the pain, and as he did so, he could see Laila's expression of misery and contempt begin to transform into something else. Her brow furrowed, not out of anger, but concern. Worry.

Yes, he thought. *Closer.*

The suffering was so awful, someone may as well have injected a cluster bomb into his head. As his body rocked back and forth in a fit of increasingly violent convulsions, the torment in every fraction of his body grew as well. Still, he kept the act up. Through the haze of dried blood and dizziness, he could make out Laila approaching in distress.

"Elijah."

The word seemed to echo endlessly in Elijah's head, as though his skull were an endless cavern.

"Elijah!" she yelled louder. Her footsteps began to pick up pace.

The shame was beginning to sink in. It wasn't enough for him to brawl with Laila and possibly give her a concussion—he just had to go and trick her like this, too.

It's justified, he thought. *I get that gun, secure my safety and hers, and then everything can get sorted out on the surface.* Still, deep down, he knew what he was doing was unforgivable.

She had finally reached his side. Her face, still battered and bruised from the punches he had delivered, was contorting in anxiety as she grabbed his shoulders and shook him around helplessly. Through the ringing in his ears, Elijah could make out her stammering, "What do I do?" over and over under her breath.

Finally, deeming it unnecessary, Elijah slowed his coughs down. With immense effort, he turned to face Laila. His body moved slowly, but his brain worked fast. He could see the glint of the gun in Laila's opposite hand.

"Elijah?"

It was as if the past fifteen minutes never happened. With her free arm, she brushed the hair out of Elijah's eyes and put two fingers to his carotid artery. She was checking his pulse.

"What happened? Are you okay?"

Elijah didn't respond. Pushing the overwhelming shame out of his mind, he painstakingly reached out a hand for Laila to grasp.

Laila, initially baffled, grabbed his outstretched hand and squeezed it.

"What's going on?" she asked again. Her hands were shaking in place as she pressed on. "Elijah, talk to me. Are you okay?"

Still, he didn't respond. He was too busy observing that the gun was still planted in Laila's opposite hand. Because his shoulder was thoroughly shattered at this point, he arduously bent his elbow so that his other hand outstretched the same way. He looked Laila in the eyes and nodded in the direction of the hand.

"No . . ." she said softly. "No, you moron. You're going to be fine. The DSRV will be here soon . . . they'll have medics aboard . . ." she tried to pull back. "You'll survive. There's no need for this."

Elijah said nothing. He simply nodded once again to his hand.

Fighting back yet another round of tears, Laila looked at Elijah, the hand, then back again. Nodding solemnly, she moved her hand to steady Elijah's.

At that precise moment, time slowed to a halt. Elijah's pained expression dropped suddenly as her gun entered view. His gaze locked onto it, causing Laila's eyes to follow. In a millisecond, his motives were elucidated.

Once she realized that he had tricked her into revealing the gun, it was too late. Elijah had already snatched his hand away from hers. His breath caught in his throat as he prepared to throw himself forward. Laila's expression shifted to one of panic, and her mouth opened as a silent scream began to emerge.

As time itself fell into slow-motion, Elijah, deciding that he had nothing left to lose, lunged one final time at the gun in Laila's hand.

Chapter Fifteen

When All is Said and Done

When Laila awoke this morning to the sound of desperate cries and clattering metal, she wasn't expecting this. Something terrible, yes. Maybe something that truly sealed her and her friends' fate for good. But not this.

In the span of five minutes, she had witnessed Rohan zip-tied and asphyxiated in a plastic bag before reluctantly turning her gun on Elijah. She couldn't believe that he had done it until he punched her in the mouth and wrestled her for the gun. This, coupled with everything else that had happened in the past few days, should've been at the forefront of her mind. But not now. All she could do was stare frozen in shock at her best friend's still body.

I didn't mean to.

The phrase echoed in her head over and over, like a yell in a deep open cavern.

I didn't mean to. I really didn't.

The last minute had been seared into her brain. She had come to comfort Elijah in what she believed to be his final moments. He was a complete disheveled mess, and she couldn't decide what was worse: the fact that one of his arms was bending the wrong way, or the fact that his wheezing seemed like it would never stop. Only when she realized that he was trying to bait her into losing the gun, did she panic. Her fingers clenched inward around the trigger, the gun kicked back violently out of her hand, and Elijah fell limp. There wasn't a dramatic moment of revelation before he collapsed. No sorrowful violins suddenly burst into song at her tragic error. He just fell back like a meaningless ragdoll and stopped breathing, leaving Laila alone to process it all.

She didn't cry. What was the point? There was no one left to cry for but herself. Instead, she slumped there, repeating the same line in her head religiously.

He grabbed at my gun, she reasoned. He beat the crap out of me just now, too. He shouldn't have done that. Why did he do that? It wasn't my fault. I didn't mean to.

Her sound reasoning didn't offer her any peace, but she continued anyway. None of it made sense. The question remained: unless Elijah had faked being a good person for over a decade, why would he suddenly murder all these people? Not that it mattered, at this point. It wasn't like she could bring him back.

As the minutes tracked by, she slowly laid herself down on her back and stared at the flickering fluorescent bulb on the ceiling.

"That's that," she whispered aloud. Her apathy wasn't working very well as a coping mechanism, but she continued regardless. "It's over."

How long until the DSRV arrives? Fifteen minutes? An hour? A day? Would it even arrive at all? Who knows. Who cares? Everyone is dead. What did it matter if she followed their lead?

A grinding noise erupted from another room down the hall. Laila brushed it off as the radio acting up again. Maybe some computer in the control room was breaking down after a week of neglect. Whatever it was, it didn't bother Laila enough to get her to stop wallowing in her own despair. The next few noises did, however.

A sliding door opened behind the second entrance to the room. There was a fit of rustling that Laila couldn't see the source of, but the sounds were strange. It didn't sound like a ventilation fan had kicked in and rustled a bunch of papers around aimlessly. No.

It sounded like footsteps.

Before she could put two and two together as to what was actually going on, a loud thumping sound appeared on the other side of the wall. After a pause, it reemerged. Then, a perfectly rectangular piece of the wall rotated aside, revealing a lightly camouflaged door. And behind it, an enormous dead man.

Laila rubbed her eyes once just to be completely sure she wasn't seeing things. When she stopped, it confirmed her worst suspicions:

he was still there. It was almost comical how absurd it was to see him in the flesh again. If she had an ounce of humanity left in her, she may have burst into laughter.

"Zach."

He smiled, not with callousness or guile. His eyes disarmed her, like a kindergarten teacher smiling knowingly at a misbehaving student. It was almost patronizing.

"Hello," he said calmly.

He walked around Laila and plucked the gun she had been carrying from under the shelf it had slid under during the brawl. For a moment, the two stood in a stalemate, waiting for the other to question how any of this was possible. Laila was the first to retire her pride and ask the question pressing on her mind.

"How?" Her voice wasn't angry anymore. She had a good idea of what her fate would be now. She just wanted an explanation.

Zach sighed and tilted his head slightly in concern.

"You're hurt," he observed. "Did you hit your head or something?"

"How?" she repeated, unamused.

The murderer took a seat on one of the intact metal rails meant to hold up the boxes of MREs. His dark gray eyes pierced through Laila as if she wasn't even there.

"How, what?" he probed. "How am I here? How did I do it all? Be more specific."

She didn't know exactly what to expect when it occurred to her that Zach was behind it all. Perhaps he would walk in and shoot her point-blank to finish the job, or maybe he'd have one of those evil villain monologues about the great injustices of the world. Somehow, his polite demeanor and pitying gaze were worse than all the rest combined. And it certainly didn't help to explain how or why he would do any of this to people like her. People like Elijah.

"Y'know, I shot my best friend because I thought he was the one who committed all those awful things you're responsible for."

Zach, surprisingly, looked taken aback.

"I'm very sorry about that," he said earnestly. After a brief pause, he continued, "but for what I was saying before, I guess you'll want to know the 'how' about everything that's happened, wouldn't you?"

"Are you going to kill me?"

Zach grinned and stood.

"I'm guessing that's a yes to the 'how' question, then. If it's not too touchy of a subject, who were the people that found me passed out?"

Laila's expression of contempt gave way to confusion.

"Passed out? You didn't have a heartbeat. You were dead."

"Nope. Passed out. From how close you and . . . hmm. Who were the others?"

At that comment, Laila began to shake with fury.

"Elijah and Rohan," she seethed.

"Yes! I remember Elijah specifically from the surface. He was a decent guy." His gaze wandered as he reminisced on those times. "Anyway, I'm sure you're aware, then, that he's a complete insomniac."

He laughed at Laila's blank stare, mistakenly believing that she didn't already know.

"Oh, so you didn't know. He has these pills, see, that knock you out for a good couple of hours. Strong, strong pills. Hell, if you take four or more on an empty stomach, you might not wake up again." He turned to wink playfully at Laila. "I should know. I almost didn't. It was infuriating trying to find where he had stashed them at first, sure, and keeping everything back in the bag was tedious as hell . . . but at the end of it, I had a way to take myself out of the game for a while. Keep everyone else running around, blaming each other for my 'death' while I take a time-out in that closet." His voice was becoming more giddy by the minute. "God, I felt so damn clever doing that."

This was all too much information for Laila to process, so she decided to take it one step at a time, lest she explode from bafflement.

"You almost didn't wake up, though. What would you have done then, smartass?"

Zach frowned at this.

"Yeah, that was an oversight on my part. You'll have to cut me some slack though; it's not like I planned this whole thing out."

Now this, THIS was news to Laila. She forced herself to sit up, despite the way it made her head swim with dizziness.

"You didn't plan all this?"

Zach stopped in place and backtracked.

"We'll come back to that. The point is, after taking care of Sebastian and taking all those pills, I woke up. Insanely dehydrated and hungry beyond all belief, but I woke up. I took a day to recover, snuck around the area for a bit to assess what had happened to everyone since I was gone, and then went right back to the closet. I knew y'all weren't coming back anytime soon. After all, why check on me when someone's been tampering with MREs?"

His expression turned solemn as he turned to face Laila head-on.

"By the way, what happened to Lars? Poor guy looked like he'd seen a ghost when he bit the dust. It's funny actually: I had something completely different planned for him, but he saved me the trouble." He smirked and shook in place, mimicking Lars' electrocution. "I never would've expected the wires to react that way. No, sir."

Enough was enough. She had gone through too much to let this monster continue to ramble without giving her a proper explanation.

"Why do any of it?" she croaked. "What did you gain? Are you a spy or something?"

He laughed uproariously in response.

"A spy?! Oh, come on, now. Really?"

In spite of everything, Laila was slightly offended by that response.

"Okay, well," she said defensively, "why else would you do all of this?"

Zach stopped laughing and pondered that question for a moment.

"I don't fully know," he admitted. "It started with Patrick, I guess. I didn't like him too much. No, sir. He would wrong me at every chance he got. I just felt like . . . like he knew something, y'know?"

"No, I don't."

Zach waved her away.

"Ah, you wouldn't. I don't expect you to, either. You haven't killed before. You don't know what it's like when people stare right through you, like they know who you are and what you can do. He is a commander, after all. He could probably recognize a killer when he saw one."

Laila couldn't fathom what she was hearing.

"So, you're a sociopath, then?"

"I guess." He brushed her off. "Anyway, he goes ahead and announces our little submarine trip. That's the kicker: we'll both be on it! Time passes, yada-yada, you get the drill. Our first night here, I sneak out of bed once all of you are asleep, and I pay a visit to the guy. I didn't expect to make it out free. I figured I'd take him out, relish in the moment, then accept whatever comes later. I'd figure it out as I went."

There were too many questions for Laila to possibly get through them all, but she was sure as hell going to try.

"So, you planned to assassinate a Navy Commander and then . . . go to jail? That's it?"

He shrugged.

"I didn't think it through much at the time. I just wanted to see the man squirm."

"Whatever, man. What happened after?" She had made the connection minutes ago that the longer she kept him talking, the longer she got to live. She'd be damned if she came all this way just to die like this.

His eyes wandered as he collected his thoughts.

"Well, Brookes came in after she heard the noise. I expected as much, so I was ready to take care of her, too. She didn't even see it coming." He frowned as he continued speaking. "It really was a shame. She was one of my favorite commanders. I'd take it back if I could.

"Regardless, I expected y'all to hear the shots and come running in to take me down. I wasn't in the mood to deal with all that, so I threw the gun beneath one of the desks and hid in the storage room on the opposite side. You guys would come, not notice my empty bed, and I'd slink back in and pretend to be just as shocked as the rest of you. That was the plan, at least. Time passed and . . . well, no one showed up. I don't know how or why, but you guys just didn't wake up. Once that became evident, I decided to head back to bed and keep up the act."

"Your only quarrel was with Patrick." Even with a throbbing headache, she could still make that connection. "Why come after all of us, then?"

At that, Zach began to grin wider and wider. There was a glimmer of insanity in his eyes as he began to pace around the room.

"That's just the thing," he agreed. "I've done this before, if you didn't know—oh, what am I kidding, of course you didn't know. It's half the reason I joined the Navy."

"Done what?" she asked, despite knowing the answer already.

"Kill."

He shook his head as though it were transparently obvious.

"I mean, duh. I would explain, but you could never understand. There's a rush you get when you catch someone by surprise. The look on their faces when they realize that this isn't a game or a joke: the look when they realize that their life is about to be cut short, by ME, no less." His hands shook as he relayed his excitement. "God, it's indescribable. It's more euphoric than any drug out there."

Laila's heart began to race faster and faster as he continued. The words tumbled out of his mouth carelessly, as though he physically couldn't contain his excitement at the prospect of taking another person's life.

He had done this before, Laila realized. *Oh, my god. I should've died a very long time ago.*

Zach, without regard for the look of abject terror on Laila's face, resumed.

"I've only done it four times. Well, three if you're only counting people. In fact, I bet you didn't even know I had a brother."

Laila winced. "Had?"

Zach just smirked.

"His name was Daniel. Boy lapped up all my parents' attention constantly, and it didn't help that he was younger than me. Out here winning cross country meets, acing all his classes, the star kid in everything he did. Me? I was the 'other' one. The one your parents get all hush-hush about when your extended family asks about you. The silver medal winner." His smile had long since faded.

"I never did well in school. I never ran fast. I was just Zach, and I thought that that'd be good enough for them. But no. As far as they were concerned, Daniel was their only child." His fists started shaking. "Seeing that, seeing all your parent's love and appreciation go to one child . . . that does something to you. You get angry. You get bitter.

"We had a forest behind our house. It wasn't incredibly expansive, but it did have a creek. My brother knew I used to love going there, so he asked to come along one day. I was smart, you see: when I saw an opportunity, I took it. So, we went. Late October, heavy winds, but we keep on pushing. He was smiling the whole time, telling me about his recent meets and asking me for advice on a girl he was planning on asking out. See, even if he was the center of attention all the time, he always treated me with dignity. He always asked about my day. I'll admit: it made what I was about to do harder. Almost made me reconsider, even. We get to the top, approach the creek, and he's staring out at the thing in wonder. 'Wow,' he says, 'I can't believe you would show me something like this!' He was lucky, in a way. The thing must've been absolutely mesmerizing, because he didn't hear me grunt as I lifted up a log and hurled it at the back of his head."

Zach paused. For the first time, a look of humanity enveloped his eyes and face. It only lasted a moment, but Laila recognized it. It was unmistakable. He continued.

"I wasn't caught. We lived in a small town, see. The police searched and searched, but they never found Daniel's body. My parents were a wreck. Their favorite child, their shining boy, was missing. I didn't mind their grief; it gave me more time to hone my skills uninterrupted. I got the formula down fast: make friends, enjoy their company for a while, then invite them on a trip into the woods. It worked like clockwork until one kid tried to fight back. Gave me a pretty good beatdown until I managed to hook an arm around his neck and take him out that way. Still, I had to go home with bloodied knuckles and a tattered face. Even if they were neglectful, my parents weren't stupid. They asked questions. Our school held assemblies on the recently missing students. Mass search-teams were assembled. I knew I had done as much as I could. I had to lay low, figure out another way to get my fix."

He turned and scowled at Laila, as though *she* were responsible for his predicament.

"I managed to hold off for *years,* you understand, years of not doing the one thing that makes me feel really, truly, alive. "Then, I shoot the two commanders, get off scot-free, and all of a sudden there's an entire catalog of people for me to kill next!" He paused his rant to take a breath and compose himself. He looked over at Laila.

"I don't need to explain all the rest to you. You know how it unfolded from there."

"So, it was all just a big game to you," she spit. "A fun little murder mystery where you get the thrill of being the one being chased."

Zach smiled warmly.

"Yeah. I tell ya, I was *this* close to being done for when Peter saw me coaxing the gun out of my bag. He wasn't even my next target, but I still had to shoot the man point-blank when all of you were awake." His face lit up as he remembered the rest. "God, I really did my best improv work after that. I usually can't force tears out that fast."

Laila was done with this.

"I see why your parents loved Daniel so much more than you. You're a piece of trash. You're sick."

Zach nodded.

"Yeah, you're probably right. Do you have any questions left?"

Laila knew exactly what that meant. A primal feeling of fear began to grow deep inside as she stared at Zach's cold dead eyes. No. She came too far for it to end like this.

"What's next for you?" she sputtered out, trying not to let her desperation show. "The DSRV comes, you get up to the surface, and there's eleven dead bodies strewn about with you as the lone survivor. How do you plan on weaseling yourself out of that, buddy?"

Zach tilted his head slightly in confusion.

"Oh. Oh, no. You misunderstand. I don't plan on going back up."

The void in Laila's stomach only grew.

"What do you mean?"

Zach scoffed and motioned around the room.

"The world's greatest manipulator couldn't explain away all this. I had a good run, I really did. I feel proud, honestly." He shrugged. "Now it's over."

Laila began to shake. "Don't say that."

"Come on." His sincerity was incredibly disturbing. "You had to have known this would happen at some point. Besides, did you really think you'd have a simple life if you made it to the surface? Your friends are dead, one of them by your own hands. You'll be paralyzed by your trauma for every waking second of your life going forward."

He twirled the gun in his hand such that the barrel pointed at Laila's eyes, unnervingly similar to her pose when she arrested Elijah.

"When you really think about it, I'm doing you a favor."

He's acting, she reasoned. *It's all a play! He'll laugh and put the gun down and let me live. He won't shoot me. Not after all of this. He . . . he couldn't.*

Deep down, though, she knew she was lying to herself. Her fate had been sealed the second she heard footsteps down the hall. Perhaps her fate had been sealed the moment one of her commanders put her on the list to go in the submarine.

But for it to end like this? No. Zach was a puppeteer—this was all just a game to him. If she could find something to offer, something to keep her alive until the DSRV arrived, everything would be okay. Her head throbbed as she attempted to come up with something witty that would get Zach to reconsider.

Yet, when she opened her mouth to speak, the words caught in her throat. She paused, cleared her throat and tried again. In a small pathetic voice, she said the only thing she could think to say.

"Please don't kill me."

This time, no reassuring smile or malicious chuckle escaped Zach. Instead, he leaned against the railing and sighed.

"Y'know, we're probably all over the news by now." He paused when he noticed Laila's baffled expression.

"I mean, come on. Think of the amount of press that a story like this would get. Daniel by himself made headlines in our entire state; a story like this would go global! Picture the headline: *'Navy boot camp loses access to submarine with twelve passengers aboard.'* I can almost guarantee that everyone's names, including yours, have been blasted on screen alongside a monochrome edit of your high school yearbook picture. Oh, and we can't forget about the sad violins in the background. You gotta have those."

"Why are you telling me all this?"

Zach shrugged again.

"Well, I figured that if you knew that you were going to be famous in your final moments, that would make this easier to do."

The instant Laila processed what that meant. It was already too late. She didn't even have time to respond before Zach's finger wrapped around the trigger.

———————

For a cramped submarine that had been the host of almost a dozen murders, everything was surprisingly tidy. Zach had only been in hiding for a day, sure, but he swore that everything was kept more organized than how he left it. The boxes were stacked neatly on top of each other in the quarters, and he couldn't find a speck of dust on any of the beds, not even the unoccupied ones.

Well, I guess they're all unoccupied now.

He paced around the rest of the submarine. There was a sense of freedom, albeit melancholic in nature, in walking around the place knowing full well that no one was around to question you or get in your way. Still, the sound of his lone footsteps echoing off the metal floor felt isolating. He may have been a murderous psycho, but even he could feel the overwhelming silence weighing in.

Finally, he passed by the control room. The juxtaposition of scattered paper and furniture to the rest of the sub was jarring at first glance. His eyebrows rose in surprise.

"What's all this?" he wondered aloud.

He picked up one of the sheets and began reading. It was a chore to decipher the page, but he began to pick up a pattern in the scribbles and scratches that made it slightly more legible. The papers were also strewn around in chronological order, and by sorting them through the hastily drawn page numbers at the bottom right of all the pages, he had sorted everything into its original cohesive order.

Who wrote all this? he wondered. *In a day or two, no less. Where'd they find the time?*

His questions were cast aside as he began to read from the beginning. It was evident from the first page that this was Elijah's work. He had a distinctive way of speaking that was reflected in what he wrote. A smile grew on Zach's face. Sure, he may have been the catalyst of Elijah's untimely and inhumane demise, but he could still show some pride in his old 'friend' and his story-telling ability thereof.

It was fascinating to read through Elijah's experiences from his own point of view. For so long, Zach had kept up the facade of being yet another helpless recruit, but for him to read what it truly felt like to be wary of death being inches away at all times . . . that was something else. Of course, Zach faced his own sense of danger every time he risked getting caught, but that was different. There wasn't a risk of mortality involved.

As he read on, the grin on his face grew wider and wider. The culmination of a week of tireless effort had paid off, and this was proof of it. He hadn't just sent the submarine into a random fit of chaos: he had actively plunged twelve people—all unwillingly—into the greatest game of cat-and-mouse the world had ever seen. And through it all—taking out the commanders, getting caught by Peter, and teetering on the edge of death through the sleeping pills—he had gone undetected until all that remained was him and Laila. His expression exploded with pride. What a beautiful performance he had thrown together.

It really is a shame that it has to end now.

Somewhat melancholically, he seized his gun from his waist and stared at it in deep thought. After dealing with Laila, he had meticulously gone to every recruit, taken their cold dead hands, and rubbed it up and down every inch of the gun, mainly the grip. It was a chore to be sure, but it was necessary if he wanted everything to end the way he wanted. Now, the world's best forensic analyst couldn't deduce with complete certainty who had used the gun the final time. Just as he did to the recruits, Zach would leave everything a mystery. He wouldn't be there to explain it all, though.

Slowly, he pressed the barrel of the gun to the back of his head, awkwardly twisted his shoulder in order to do so. To any crime scene investigator, it would look as though he were shot from behind, although by whom would remain a mystery.

The cold metal sent a shiver down his spine as he rested his finger on the trigger. He shut his eyes tightly as his brain raced to ensure he hadn't skipped over any crucial steps. Everyone's fingerprints on the gun: check. Radio busted beyond repair: check. Everything was set in place.

There was only one loose end now.

It seemed that every time Lieutenant Arnold needed a coaster to place his cup of tea on, it was nowhere to be found. He was convinced this kind of thing would only happen when his work was a mess, and this time was no exception. He danced around, his cup swaying in his other hand as he searched. Sunlight peered from the window of his office and brightened the dim corners of the room. The compound had been in chaos for the past few days, and he was the only one left to pick up the pieces. His mind raced with thoughts; after all, there was a lot to do.

In the past six hours, information from the DSRV team had come through. They had located the hijacked submarine, and despite their best efforts on the other side, nobody was coming to unlock the hatch. Fearing the worst, they had breached by force and searched the inside. It was official: no one survived.

It wasn't enough that Arnold had to organize a search squad, investigative team, and now a funeral service in the span of a week. He had failed to protect a dozen innocent people, two of whom were his own colleagues. Now, he couldn't even sit down to begin drafting the letters to the parents of the deceased, not without a coaster to put his cup on.

There was rapping at the door.

"Lieutenant Arnold, sir! Open the door, please!"

"If it's the goddamn press again, don't give them any information." He kicked his chair out of the way furiously. "I've had enough of them for a lifetime."

"Sir, it's not the press, sir."

"Well, whoever or whatever it is, it can wait five minutes."

Arnold held in a yelp as a drop of boiling tea fell on his thumb. Of course, there wasn't a coaster for him to put it down on. Why on earth would there be? Why would the universe give him a break? He thought of the parents he'd have to talk to. *God, I've only been here for two years,* he thought. He figured it would have to take—"

"Lieutenant Arnold!"

"IN A MINUTE!"

Arnold had given "the news" to grieving parents before. It's all part of the job description, he supposed. But damn it, ten recruits?

Ten of their brightest, best performing recruits? He recognized their names the second news came out that their submarine was off the radar. Laila Walker. Lars Hall. The Leagues. He was fond of them all. Hell, even Zachary King was in there. He was the brightest for sure. What kind of world would take students like those?

"LIEUTENANT!!"

The teacup had left his hands before he had even registered what he had done. It slammed into the wall on the opposite side of the room, sending dozens of shards of glass careening every which way. The tea began to drip unevenly from the point of impact, spilling onto the white carpet beneath him. The photos and certificates on the wall were streaked with brown now.

Arnold cracked his knuckles and sighed. His mind wasn't preoccupied with the cleanup in the least. He stepped over the damage he made and opened the door to a frantic and slightly dazed Officer Zane. He was carrying a briefcase.

"What was that?"

"Nothing," Arnold said while gesturing at the doorway. "You just come in here and tell me what the hell is so important."

"Oh," Zane said before plopping the case down on the table, scattering a calculator and pens in the process. "It's very important, otherwise I wouldn't have—"

"Just get on with it."

"Right." He reached around the end and unclipped the case, revealing a stack of stained, torn, but still faintly legible paper. He turned back to Arnold.

"Are you familiar with Elijah Smith?"

"He was one of the submarine recruits," Arnold answered. "I was just about to write to his mother and father to let them know that their little boy is dead."

Zane didn't flinch.

"Sir, I completely understand how awful this is. No one, not one recruit or officer can sit still right now. I get it. But it's important to me that you listen right now."

Arnold threw his hands up.

"You haven't given me much reason to focus on this instead of the million other tasks I have."

"Listen," Zane said. "I was present when the DSRV came up. I got this case from the crew myself. Apparently, they found a series of written entries, some chronicling day-by-day events down in the submarine."

"Sorry?"

"Elijah was writing about everything going on, WHILE it was going on. These are the papers here." He gestured in the direction of the briefcase. "We're incredibly lucky they're still in the condition they're in."

Arnold stood, legs shaking slightly as he moved over the briefcase. Zane put a hand up to stop him from going much farther.

"The contents of this case are distressing, nauseating, all as you'd expect. But it's also incredibly enlightening. This is something that should take priority right now. The children are going to stay dead, and so will CDR Patrick and Brookes. The letters to their families can be completed by another officer. But this? This is our best shot at understanding what happened to them. It's your job to decode it. Elijah's laid it all out."

"I don't understand." Arnold's voice shook as processed it all. "How?"

"I'll give you time with it." Zane softly pushed the briefcase forward.

With a reassuring pat on Arnold's shoulder, he stepped over the now-dry carpet and began pacing out of the room. He stopped right before the exit and turned.

"Sir?"

Arnold turned around, light-headed.

"What is it, Zane?"

"You might want to sit down."

ABOUT THE AUTHOR

Tanay Pant is a student who lives with his family and dog in Illinois. He has been writing for as long as he can remember, starting out with scrappy comic books made out of notebook paper before completing *Connection Terminated*, his second published novel.

In his spare time, he enjoys writing for the school newspaper, playing sports with his friends, or listening to music a bit louder than he should.